Vendetta

Simon Pert

Bright Pen

Visit us online at www.authorsonline.co.uk

A Bright Pen Book

Text Copyright © Simon Pert 2011

Cover design by © David Stooke
www.davidstooke.co.uk

British Library Cataloguing Publication Data.
A catalogue record for this book is available from the British Library

ISBN 978-0-7552-1421-1

Authors OnLine Ltd
19 The Cinques
Gamlingay, Sandy
Bedfordshire SG19 3NU
England

This book is also available in e-book format, details of which are available at www.authorsonline.co.uk

To Nina, Ella and Taylor - always x

Acknowledgements

There are many people I have to thank who helped in varying ways with this book and at different stages of its life, but simply put, without them the book may never have seen the light of day. To Jo Ratcliffe, thank you for taking the time to read and edit from the beginning of this project and to allow me to run ideas by you (even when they were bad ideas!) and to those of you who read early drafts of the novel and whose comments gave me the push I needed to carry on with the story, I am eternally grateful.

To Paul Cude and his lovely family, thank you for refocusing my writing and giving me that all important nudge to get on with it.

To Rachel Cude a big thank you for your editing job, and to David Stooke who designed my front cover, an amazing artist, thank you so much.

Thanks as ever to my family who as always give me unabashed encouragement despite my obvious enjoyment for writing about crime and death!

And to those of you who are reading this book, I simply say thank you…

Now lock the doors and check the windows, pull up a chair and turn the page…it's time to begin…

S

Prologue:

December 2nd 1985

Despite the warmth of his office, Dr Robert Fox couldn't dispel the chill that had descended over the office. The coolness was seeping through his clothes, nibbling at his flesh like a hungry parasite. Standing in front of the window, he gazed absently out towards the greying afternoon sky at the slender waif-like figure of the blonde haired girl who only moments ago had been a patient seated in his office. She had been his patient for six months, six months of virtual silence, of closed in contempt. An eleven year old girl with a vehement rage that was bubbling beneath the surface, yet she seemed adamant about keeping it there, unwilling to take the help or guidance offered to her.

Until today, that was!

Today she had spoken, freely and generously, without restraint. Her words were cold and unemotional. Whilst at the same time they chilled him to his very core. More so because they were being spoken from the tongue of someone so young, a minor in the eyes of the law, a girl still steeped in childhood. Yet inside of her there raged a bitterness he had not seen in one so young. A resentment so full of hostility. A young girl so unreceptive to the offer of help, the olive branch that was being held out towards her. In his twenty years working with problematic children he had never met one so young and so full of darkness.

Fox had been unprepared, he berated and he silently scolded himself for his professional gullibility despite his years of experience. He had expected the normal round of silence mixed with sulkiness. The averted eyes, the twisting of hands, squeezing her pale, fragile looking hands into fists. He expected what he had been given before; the obvious discomfort at being in his presence, in his office once more, of a man prying into her past, doing his best to understand her present with a view to helping her forge a future.

Yet her words, when at first she had spoken, offered him hope, suggested that inside there was still a little girl wanting to be saved. Wishing for someone to take the pain and the anger and the bitterness and wash it all away.

He was wrong.

The girl disappeared from sight, her slender frame swallowed by the red double-decker bus that passed by. All that was left was the greying sky, the falling rain and the chilling sense of unease that was spreading like a cancer within him.

He thought of his wife, Judy, who was a probation officer in child services. Should he tell her, should he confide and break that most sacred of vows: confidentiality? Should he divulge his fears and his apprehension, his trepidation and dread of what might happen? Dr Robert Fox had a feeling that the girl who had just left his office was beyond redemption even at such a young age. What troubled him more, what nagged at the very back of his mind like a nightmarish critter that waits until the room is dark before spooking the sleeping child, was the fact that he knew the girl was a ticking time bomb but could do nothing to prevent the fallout or help her.

The words she had spoken chilled him each time they replayed themselves inside his mind like his Sony Walkman VM-W800. The thought of the present that his wife had bought him not long ago drew his eyes from the outside world and across the room to his desk where his Walkman sat. He crossed the room and sat down in his chair, grabbed the headphones and slipped them over his head. He had been listening to Bruce Springsteen's Born To

Run cassette, was on side two listening to the title track. Pressing the play button he tried to let the gravelly vocals drown out the thoughts that were rattling around the insides of his skull.

It didn't work.

Still the girl's voice and words were there, repeatedly echoing.

"I will kill them for what they have done to me..."

Article that appeared in The Daily Chronicle
Friday 6th December 1985

Police are asking the public
for help in order to catch
the killer of Dr Robert Fox,
who on Tuesday evening was
stabbed to death in what
police are describing as a vicious,
brutal and unprovoked attack.
Anyone with information has
been asked to contact Detective
Inspector Brian Lewis on…

Chapter 1

The night was bitterly cold as the man stirred, awakened from his disorganised and chaotic dreams by a movement close by. He opened blurred and hazy eyes but could distinguish little in the darkness that swamped his chosen domicile. The man called himself Dennis but was known in homeless circles as Denny. He had a mass of grey hair and a beard of the same colouring. His face was lined and his eyes were dark unfathomable circles in an otherwise aged and somewhat haunted face. It was the face of a man who had lived a life less ordinary, the face of a man who had secrets, perhaps dark secrets.

He moved slightly, trying to make as little noise as possible.

Then he saw the small pinpoint of light heading his way.

His body stiffened as a voice called out quietly to him. A new kind of cold seeped through his clothing and his makeshift bedding, the kind of cold that only a haunted past and the knowledge of imminent death can bring.

The light disappeared.

Everything returned to darkness, to silence, to nothing, to normality. He became swamped by the darkness once more, just the way he liked to live his life, on the periphery, hidden in the shadows, away from the prying of eyes and the olive branch of kindness.

Was I dreaming? Denny asked himself. When no other sound, save for the distant reaches of traffic moving through the city and the occasional barking dog played in his ears, he laid his head back down and closed his eyes. The nightmares that were his past returned to haunt him as they did on a regular, almost daily basis. He had never realised that it was possible to have nightmares during the day whilst you were awake, but he knew different now. His past followed him like a chain around his neck, a noose waiting to be tightened; a chain of guilt that he knew was wholly deserved. What was worse he knew that there was no path to redemption, no way to cleanse the soul of past transgressions. There was, quite simply, no way to make better what he had done all those years ago.

It was then, as the vaults that held back the memories of yesteryear threatened to crack, to spew forth their clandestine truths, that the hands gripped his throat; tight and strong the gloved hands squeezed harder and harder....

In all his years of living rough, of surviving the battle of the elements, harsh winters and hot warm summers, of avoiding beatings by the drunk and the brutal, he had wondered time and time again if the notion of seeing your life flash before your eyes before it was extinguished forever, was a fallacy or not.

As the gloved hands squeezed tighter and tighter he found the floodgates of his past rip wide open quickly followed by memories and images that had been lost to time and circumstance.

As the realisation dawned on what would soon be his last breath, Denny felt a tear sting his dirtied cheeks, his last thoughts of the daughter he had let down, the daughter he had always wanted to find but had never had the guts to look for.

With one last breath darkness descended over staring eyes.

The past had caught up and would soon become an unrelenting animal, dangerously out of control.

The gloved hands released the body and let it fall back towards its make-shift bed, there was more to be done, but for a moment the assailant was happy to revel in his work.

Chapter 2

They had eaten well at the restaurant by the river. Having shared a bottle of white Merlot, they had enjoyed a meal of Butternut and Spinach Risotto and Baked Shrimp in Tomato Feta sauce before rounding off with a shared Pannacotta. Their conversation had been easy, light and uncomplicated. With appetites satisfied and the bill settled (David had insisted on paying despite an offer to go Dutch) they took a slow walk along the river path at Margaret's request.

The sky was clear of cloud and the full moon shone brightly, whilst the rain and wind that had been aggressive in its assault during the previous weekend appeared to be on the decline, leaving in its trail a rare pleasant evening for the middle of January.

Feeling David take her hand in his, Margaret heard the sound of his voice but paid hardly any attention to his words. She was in her own little world. She was happy, content, and not just because the dinner had gone so well; she was excited. Excited by the anticipation of what was yet to come.

They paused to watch the river. Hardly a ripple disturbed the surface. Across from them they heard the far off sound of traffic mingled with the muffled sound of music and chatter from a bar on the other side of the river. A chorus of Happy Birthday was being enthusiastically sung and, for a brief moment, she revelled in the sound of the music and the laughter that emanated from the building and wondered, not for the first time, why it was that the idea and practice of enjoyment was so alien to her. A familiar rage began to build but she contained it, now was not the time, now was the time for David, everything else could wait for a little while.

The path beside the river walk was deserted, much like the restaurant had been. Diners were obviously not akin to eating out so soon after the accumulation of Christmas and New Year, an indulgence whilst they waited for the arrival of the January payday and obligatory credit card statements.

The couple continued their post dinner stroll, each lost within their own thoughts of what was to come, of what would happen, how it would happen.

Margaret turned, her mouth poised to utter something when the man leapt out at them from the shadows of the bridge.

He stood still for a second; the dark figure lit eerily by moonlight showing his tall body, his hair pulled back in a ponytail with paint splattered jeans and a torn top. His arms were exposed, despite the cold, to show a series of painted images that started at his wrist and became lost to his shoulders and beyond. He stood before them, looming like an apparition; whilst the couple froze. Margaret felt the tension in David as his body stiffened and he gripped her hand tighter.

'Can you help me?' The man cried, jumping from the grass verge and disappearing down towards the river, seconds later the splash of water sounded deafening in the still of the night. 'There's a body in the river and I can't get it out by myself, it's caught at the edges.'

David exchanged a glance with Margaret, but he had already let his hand slip from her and was advancing forward, removing his jacket.

'Wait!' she said, fear and apprehension in her tone.

'It's okay.' David replied, already at the edge of the grassy verge.

'What if he's faking, what if he…' her words were drowned out as she heard the sound of the water's surface broken for the second time in as many minutes. She edged closer to the river bank to try and get a look at what was happening. A few moments later both appeared as they hauled the dark form from the river, before collapsing on the grass verge where they both fell for a moment, exhausted, cold, wet and shaking, trying to catch their rasping breath.

'Is he dead?' The stranger asked, as he looked to David who was crouching at the body's side, hands quickly searching for a pulse.

'Have you got a phone?' David shouted. 'Dial 999 and hurry.'

The man looked to the scared woman standing on the path.

'I don't have a mobile. Miss, do you have one?' Rejuvenated, Margaret dug her hand into her bag and pulled out her phone quickly dialling for the emergency services, all the while keeping an eye on the tall, gangly looking man with the ponytail and arms covered in tattoos.

'I think we're too late.' David said after a few moments as he joined Margaret and the stranger on the footpath, all three gazing down at the deceased man, while in the distance the sound of approaching sirens gave rise to the finality of the situation they found themselves in.

The police were quick to arrive and took charge.

They took statements and collected contact details before letting them go.

As David guided her away from the river path toward the taxi rank, Margaret caught sight of the tattooed man's face.

He smiled at her.

She winked at him, his job was done.

Her work was just beginning

* * *

She opened her eyes with a start.

What had woken her? Pushing her body up on her elbows, Margaret looked across to the man sleeping soundly next to her. She relaxed a little, eased her breathing, and pushed the covers away from her warm body. In the combination of moonlight and streetlamps outside she crossed the room and slipped into her underwear before pulling on her shirt that was strewn across a chair. Having quickly dressed she left the bedroom.

She felt groggy but pleased. She felt like a hibernating animal who had slept for winter and was now ready to engage with the world once more.

She crossed to the kitchen and took a glass from the draining board, opened the bottle of Jack Daniels from the side and poured herself a small measure. She took the drink across to the window that looked down over the side street below.

Leaning against the window, watching the pools of water shimmer with the reflection of the streetlamps, Margaret took a drink, savouring the burning sensation in her throat.

Come the morning David would wake to an empty bed. If he tried to call her mobile all he would get would be a disconnected number, if he tried to email he would get a bounce back message. In short, she would disappear, it was something she was good at doing, she had done it so many times before and for a variety of reasons. She would reinvent herself, she always did, a chameleon of her own making.

Draining the remainder of the drink she returned the glass to the kitchen counter and went through to the bedroom, crawled into bed and playfully nudged the sleeping man in the back.

'Sorry, didn't mean to wake you,' she said as David was hauled from the recesses of sleep.

'You okay?' he asked, sleep combining with concern.

'Just had a nightmare that was all,' she said, over-exaggerating the expression of unease. When David pulled her into his arms, she buried her face into his chest concealing the satisfied smile etched over her features. Before leaving she wanted what was hers to take, and like everything else in life, she knew how to get it and the right buttons to press.

Tomorrow was another day, and with that brought about the next stage of her plan, the promise of the next target on her vendetta list.

As her lips nibbled at his chest and whilst her hand slipped beneath the covers her mind was already racing ahead of itself, her mind devouring ideas like a hungry animal.

She thought back to one of her former therapists, Robert Fox, and wondered if he knew what he had set in motion all those years ago. How it was that his constant questions, his probing, his need to help fix someone that society had deemed broken, had unleashed the design, the blueprint, for a plan that was now beginning in earnest.

Chapter 3

George Soderman sat at his desk with a pile of scattered papers covering the teak coloured desk top. He felt frustrated by the lack of progress, irritated by the barriers that kept parading themselves in front of him. Deciding that he could do no more this evening, he returned some printed emails and an updated report back in to the brown folder and cast it aside.

It was as he let his weary body lean back in the chair that he heard the sound of the front door bell ring.

He stared up at the clock that hung over the door wondering who in their right mind would visit at this time of night. His annoyance was quickly replaced by a curiosity that had followed him from youth and into a flourishing career as an academic professor of English and English Literature, although now several years retired. As he listened to the sound of the door buzzer reverberating for a second time, he got up from behind his desk with a groan of frustration and made his way towards the front door.

Most of his closest friends and acquaintances lived out of town and most knew better than to just turn up unannounced. Many times he had ignored the buzz of the doorbell to save being disturbed from his work.

He switched on the outside light and leant close to the door, his hands against the key.

'Who is it?' he asked, trying to mask the sound of unease tinged with a hint of curiosity.

'Dad!' came the rather weak reply. The retired professor wasted no time in turning the key and yanking the bolts from the top and bottom of the door. Quickly he opened the front door, and there on the front step stood his daughter, Natalie.

Her face was pale, frightened, her eyes glassy and full of tears and without saying another word she collapsed into his arms, burying her head into his shoulder, sobbing into his dressing gown. George Soderman simply stood there, his hand stroking the back of her dark hair, a flood of emotions rushing through him like a tidal wave through a broken dam.

As he held her, her sobs gradually subsiding, he marvelled for the countless time, how much she looked like his late wife in her youth.

Suddenly the young woman seemed to have reverted to that little girl of yesteryear, as though all the years in-between had been nothing but a dream, swept aside by the tide of time. Keeping his arms wrapped tightly clasped around her, he wondered when he had last held her so tightly. In the doorway of what had once been the family home they remained locked together, the abnormally warm evening of earlier giving way to a winter chill that nipped at their skin. While Natalie seemed oblivious to the coldness that streamed through the front door, her father was the opposite. Beneath his clothing the wintry evening left a trail of goose bumps across his skin.

George Soderman kissed the top of his daughter's head, the aroma of blueberry scented shampoo filling his senses. He smiled, waiting for his daughter's body to stop shuddering, waiting for her to calm herself. Only then could he try and understand what had brought her to his doorstep and in a state such as this.

* * *

Natalie sat at the kitchen table with the yellow and white gingham tablecloth, fruit bowl and fresh flowers. It was as though her late mother was still here, such was the attention to detail and design that remained some five years since George Soderman and his daughter had laid Mary to rest.

It was also the same kitchen table that had seen her graduate from the little girl lost who would labour for hours over her colouring books with their promise of fairies and princesses; through those heady days of learning to write, copying text that her father had written down for her, through the exam studies and culminating in the professional woman who had now returned to sit at the same table.

A stab of guilt stole the smile of recollection from her face, it had been some six months since she had been here last, six months in which she had grabbed snatches of telephone conversation with her father mingled with his occasional visits to London where they would grab a coffee in Starbucks on Tottenham Court Road or, as they had done the last time he had visited, a coffee and sandwich from one of the refreshment points in Hyde Park before losing themselves within the grounds for as long as they could, for as long as time allowed.

She watched as her father poured two mugs of coffee before joining her on the opposite side of the table.

'My doctor would have a fit if he knew I was drinking coffee this late at night.' He joked, doing his best to lighten the mood. 'It's not every day your very own daughter drops by unannounced, so what's happening? I spoke to you only this morning.' This was true enough, Natalie had rung her father not long after landing back on English soil, returning from her trip to Paris. 'You sounded okay then, what changed?'

'Smoke and mirrors, maybe, false smiles, however you want to dress it up.' Natalie replied, not looking up from her coffee to meet what she knew would be there staring at her, her father's inquisitive and probing concerned eyes.

'What would you have done if I hadn't been here?' he asked matter-of-factly, changing the subject for the moment, in no rush to force anything from his daughter. He knew her too well, and in her own time she would open up, but not before. He stared at her dark hair that she kept pushing away from her face as though it agitated her. She looked pale and ashen, even more so than normal, and again he wondered what trouble had landed at her door, what dark spectre of the modern world had been circling and finally crashed down upon terra firma.

'I would have used the key.'

'What key?'

'The one you keep in the hanging basket on the side of the garage.' Natalie said with a smile.

'Oh that one, I suppose I really should remember not to leave it there, especially with the way the world is these days but old habits seem to die hard.'

'If mum was here she...' Natalie stopped what she was saying and flashed a guilty look at her father who merely smiled sympathetically back.

'If your mother was here she wouldn't be concerned about the key moreover she would want to know what was going on with you. She would also know exactly what to say to you, whereas I, unfortunately, am still ill at ease in navigating the waters of your problems, especially when I don't know what has happened to land you, albeit it gladly, on my doorstep so late at night.' He smiled as he finished, showing that there was no animosity just concern for his little girl.

A brief silence fell between them, leaving only the sounds of the house – the ticking of the kitchen clock, the occasional tapping of skeletal branches on the kitchen window, the creak and groan of an ageing house at the end of the day. George Soderman drank the remnants of his coffee, stood up and crossed to the butler's sink to wash out his cup. It always amazed Natalie how he drank his hot drinks so quickly, she had always affectionately called him asbestos mouth but now didn't seem the time for humour as she opened up to her father and told him what had happened earlier in the day.

When she had finished regurgitating the contents of her tale, the path that had led to her unannounced arrival on his doorstep, her father looked at her with unspoken questions, as if he were contemplating what to say before the words left his mouth.

'So they have no idea when it happened?' George Soderman asked as he sat back down at the kitchen table.

'My neighbour said that she noticed the door open last night, went and got her husband who checked the place out and then called the police.'

'Didn't they try and call you?'

'I hadn't got around to giving them my new number; I changed phone numbers six months back when I was getting those strange phone calls. Anyway, I just didn't want to stay in the house on my own, especially as whoever did this did a great job of trashing everything. And besides, I was going to call you and see if it was okay to visit at the weekend anyway, I'm just a few days early that's all.'

'Guess so. Have you got anything with you?'

'I have my bag that I took to Paris and I managed to pack a few other items into a second bag before leaving, or at least some things that hadn't been trashed.'

'Give me the keys and I'll go fetch them in for you.'

'You don't have to do that.'

'I know I don't have to, but I want to. Besides, you are, and always will be, my baby girl so why don't you go and have a shower or run a bath and try and relax and try and put what happened out of your mind even if only for a few moments.'

'As long as you're sure?'

'Yes I'm sure, now get going.'

'In that case then I think I will go and grab a quick shower.' Knowing that it was useless to argue with her father she handed over the car keys and watched as he headed towards the front door.

'Have you eaten yet?' he called from the hallway.

'Not yet.'

'In that case whilst you're having a shower I'll rustle us up some food.'

'Honestly…'

'Hell, I've had coffee now; I'll be awake for hours anyway.' With that Natalie heard him chuckling to himself before heading out of the front door. She smiled to herself, loving the sound of his laughter; it had always made her feel better, always made her feel safe and secure no matter what personal drama she was going through at the time. It was the same feeling she had when she returned home to the place of her childhood, the only place she had ever really grown up in.

It was a place she had spent so many happy years living in, a place where so many happy memories had been created. Then she thought of her flat in London and of the mess it was currently in, of the state the person or persons responsible had left it in; the thought brought tears to the brink of spilling over but she did her best to hold them in check.

Hearing the sound of her car alarm being deactivated, Natalie stood up, took her mug to the sink and headed for that long hot shower that was waiting.

She paused on the threshold of her father's study, a place in childhood that had always been out of bounds, a restricted adults only environment, the ultimate no go room. In later years he had relaxed and Natalie had spent some time in there with her father and his array of books. Peeking inside now she saw a mass of papers littered over the desk. She crossed to it and idly glanced at the papers and open books that constituted more or less a mess, not that her father would see it that way. He would always describe his desk as organised chaos, nothing more and certainly nothing less. Natalie was pretty much the same; her desk at work was in a similar state of continual chaos.

A name scrawled down on a piece of paper caught her eye. Leaning forward she took a closer look and noticed that the name was repeated again, this time on a typed letter, several typed letters in fact.

'I see you still have your mother's touch for being nosy,' said the voice from behind her, its tone touched with humour and warmth. Natalie jumped, startled by her father's voice and more so his speed at bringing the bags inside. As her body jerked she found herself knocking some of the papers to the floor. She rushed to tidy them but her father laughed affectionately, told her to leave them, and then followed her out of the study as she made her way towards the stairs that led towards her old bedroom. Her father followed gingerly behind her carrying her two travel bags.

Standing in the room that had seen her progress from child to adult, a room where dreams had been born, and reduced to rubble before being born again, Natalie felt a surge of emotion overcome her. Her father noticed and put the bags down before wrapping her in his arms and hugging her until her tears dried and her body had stopped shaking.

'I'll go and fix something to eat, you just take as long as you like and come down when you're ready, you hear me?' Planting a kiss on her forehead and giving her a final squeeze of comfort, George Soderman left, leaving Natalie to her old bedroom and the shower that was waiting to try and rinse the day's events away.

Sinking down upon the bed she felt a guiltiness rush through her. She was open with her father about most things. She had told him about the freak phone calls she had started to receive, how no voice ever spoke, yet she had the sensation that someone was on the other end. At first she had tried to ignore the calls, putting them down to teenage pranks, acts of juvenile delinquents or those of a crank. But the more she had ignored them the more they came until finally she had had to change her number. A frustrating and expensive change, but a much needed one, and one that had worked, since then she had received no more crank calls.

What she hadn't told her father about was that last month she had been attacked whilst on her way home, about how she had been dragged from the pavement into the bushes by her hair and subjected to a humiliation that bordered nearly on rape but that thankfully had stopped short from that final awfulness and resulted only in cuts, bruises and a few days of rest. The inner mental bruising was still healing though, and would continue to do so.

What was it they say about bad things happening in threes? she mused, trying to push the assault from her mind. Lying back on the bed, Natalie wondered for the umpteenth time if the break-in was the final act in the three part tragedy. If all bad things happened in threes, surely this must be the last? She hoped so at any rate.

* * *

George Soderman hurried to his study and gathered all the papers that had fallen to the floor, the ones with the names on that he didn't want his daughter to see. Oh she had seen the name of Harrison Stone, he was quite sure of that, it was probably the reason she was leaning in close to read the papers, but he didn't think that she would remember the name, especially since it was close to twenty-five years since they had last seen one another.

Despite that, he piled all the letters and the folder into his desk drawer, locked it and put the key into his trouser pocket.

Then he hurried through to the lounge and took a newspaper from the table, flipped through to the third page and scanned the article that was printed. It was to do with the death of a homeless man in the city a few nights back, the name in the article stated that the man was called Dennis but was known locally as Denny to all who knew him.

The man may have been many years older, may have gained a little weight, his mane of hair mostly grey, but Soderman knew that the likeness did not end there. The body that had been pulled from the river was most certainly that of Henry Glover despite the name of Dennis "Denny" Thomas being given. Henry Glover, a man who thirty years ago, had been suspected of assaulting multiple women, although no proof had ever been found to convict him. He had spent time inside for burglary and handling stolen goods. He was a man who avoided work wherever possible. He was a man who had friends in low places.

Henry Glover was Natalie's blood father.

Some things were best left buried, George Soderman mused. But in the back of his mind the tiny voice of apprehension spoke, *Everything comes to the surface eventually*. It was a sentiment that George did not want to consider at that exact moment, the truth scared him too much.

Chapter 4

Harry Stone headed back to the office, unsure why instead of heading for home; it seemed the office made more sense, a place he knew well, a place that was his sanctuary against the world, unlike his home that still had a lot of his belongings packed inside cardboard boxes.

He unlocked the door and disabled the alarm system, went into his office and collapsed in his chair. He could still catch the faint lingering scent of Sara's perfume, the sweet flowery aroma of Lady Million that she had been wearing that evening. The perfume, coupled with the remembrance of her lips brushing his cheek as they had parted later in the evening, made his heart ache. Sara had looked good, was happy with life. She had told Harry that she wasn't dating anyone, but then he wondered if maybe she was sparing his feelings or perhaps didn't want to share that kind of intimacy with him now that they were no longer seeing one another.

They had had dinner at a local bar and grill in which he had stolen sneaky glances at her. He had noted the new haircut and clothes, gone was the shoulder-length hair, now it was cut into a trendy bob. She had lost weight, not that she had needed to, but she had told him that she had started going swimming twice a week and to the gym three times. Again Harry wondered if this was all for herself or perhaps for a new man, maybe he would find out one day, maybe she would tell him or perhaps he would bump into the couple in town.

As always after one of their catch-ups he tried to give the impression of coolness, of aloofness, that she no longer mattered to him in any significant way, but it was just an act, an obvious lie. The stolen glances were enough of a giveaway, let alone the sense of loss when she was gone. He knew that there was little or no chance of the relationship ever being resurrected, just as he knew in his heart of hearts that he had to move on, that he needed to move on. He also knew that he would spend the next couple of days in a lethargic mood of self-loathing and self-berating. Harry knew that it had been his fault that the relationship had ended, he had been the one to blame; he was the one who had ruined the relationship, not the other way around. That old adage of time being a great healer, in this case, was a complete fallacy. He regretted the day that Sara had walked out of their life together, always would, but more than that, he hated the way that he had let her go without so much as a fight to save what they had once had. At the same time he couldn't blame her for moving on with her life, after all she wanted the whole deal. She wanted the wedding, children, the family home bustling with laughter and the chaos that children inevitably would have brought. Harry on the other hand didn't want to be woken up in the middle of the night to change a nappy or to worry every time his son or daughter went out that they wouldn't come to any harm, that they would be good rounded kids who knew when you had to walk away from danger.

Thoughts of family, albeit one that would never come to fruition, brought his mind and recollections to his own family. To his mother who had passed away some eighteen months ago after a lingering illness that had been kept from her only son. He thought of his sister Charlotte, who had disappeared in the summer of nineteen-ninety-four. There had been, and still were, many theories of what had happened to her, had she run away on her own or maybe with a boyfriend, had she been taken by someone of a depraved nature? Was she alive or dead? Harry couldn't help but feel that everyone who had ever been close to him had somehow left him. He made a mental note to ring his father tomorrow; it had been a while since he had last seen him.

On his desk next to his phone sat a small six by four photo frame with a postcard of a sunny beach scene that covered the glass front. The postcard had been from his assistant who had travelled to Australia last year to visit her daughter. Leaning forward he removed the image of the sandy beach and gazed over the black and white picture of Sara. It had been taken whilst they were holidaying in Cornwall on a day when, amazingly for the UK, the sun had been shining, the weather warm but not hot and their romance had been in its first stages of infancy. Sara sat in a lazy chair with her knees pulled up to tuck against her; she was wearing her favourite baggy grey jumper, one that he had bought for her only the week before. The smile on her face was of better times, happier times, contented times. It was a smile he knew well, a smile he missed, and a smile that he knew was gone for ever.

Harry stared at the picture lost in thought. Perhaps it was time to put it away, he thought, deciding against it for the moment. Thinking that it was better to concentrate his mind on something instead of labouring in the past, Harry Stone replaced the postcard and switched on his computer monitor, unlocked the screen with his password before loading the company database system.

He brought up his latest batch of jobs and quickly ran through the current status of each of them. Most were in a state of limbo. Most of his private investigation jobs dealt with missing persons, unfaithful spouses or, as of late, teenage children subjected to bullying gangs either in person or by means of social media websites.

As he clicked on job number four-hundred and three he glanced at the time on the computer screen. It was just after 10pm, late for some, but for this client it was normal practise to engage in telephone conversations at this stage of the evening.

Despite the four glasses of wine he had had with dinner Stone felt clear headed and alert, he always did when he was working. Picking up his telephone handset he dialled the number and waited. When the answer phone kicked in, the first time this had ever happened with this client, Stone stumbled over his words but finally left a simple message.

'Hi George it's Harry Stone here, just wanted to catch-up on recent events and give you a progress report, not that there is much to report. I'll give you a ring tomorrow.' With that he put down his phone and clicked on the attachments section of the screen, a section that held all scanned copies of documents that Harry held on the case. One of the scanned images was of Natalie Soderman, a girl he had not seen in some twenty years. She was still hauntingly beautiful with her raven hair and eyes that looked, even then, like they held something of both promise and mystery.

Of course this case, unlike his normal run of the mill caseload, was strictly between himself and George Soderman, nothing was to get back to Natalie. Stone clicked on another attachment, this one showed a younger girl, same hair style but this one blonde instead of dark. But it was eyes that Stone focussed on; the girl's eyes were darker, empty somehow, maybe they would even be described as sinister. As though whatever it was that was going on behind them was for her mind only and no one else was being let in to her world.

Harry felt a shiver encase his body.

He heard a noise in the hallway outside of his office.

Strange, he thought, no one is normally around at this time of the night, even the cleaners were normally gone by 9pm at the latest. The company who leased the offices above were, for the most part, a nine-to-five outfit; very rarely did they work beyond 6pm.

With that he closed down the two attachments and locked his screen.

He still heard movement.

'Hello?' he called out but no response came. Finally he reached the outer door that led into the entrance hall of the building. With breath held, he counted down from three and then pulled open the door with a rush of boldness that surprised the investigator.

* * *

Paul Williams shut off his computer, grabbed his keys and did a last check of doors and windows before alarming the office and heading down the stairs. He checked his watch and inwardly felt a sense of foreboding. His kids would be in bed and his wife would not be pleased that yet again he had been disturbed at home and had to head into town to check why one of the alarm systems had been triggered at the office.

How hard was it to shut a door or close a window and enter a four digit code into a panel, surely a trained monkey of any kind could manage that, he thought, pausing outside of the door that led into the offices of Hunter Stone and co.

Earlier, after returning from the building across the road that had caused his return, he had been looking for his keys when Harry Stone had ripped open the door and confronted him as though he were trying to break in. Both men had cracked a smile when they realised how ridiculous it was that both grown men had been spooked by one another.

Stone and Williams had become good friends over the past few years, and especially during the last twelve months they had taken to meeting for a coffee, normally towards early evening when others were heading for the door off home, or on the odd occasions family or work commitments didn't offer any resistance, they would go for a beer. They shared the same interest and taste in music, enjoyed trading insults and sparring linguistically over their respective football teams – Williams was a keen Liverpool red, whilst Stone was an occasional Gunner.

Williams, despite liking the man, found Stone to be an odd character. He never seemed to speak of close family, friends or mention any girlfriend. Aside from their chats about music and sport Stone appeared to be a loner, a solitary man. To outsiders who didn't know him, he was portrayed as a workaholic and an insomniac at best; whilst to those who were allowed into his inner circle, however briefly, they saw the investigator as a man who was a crusader for the missing and a habitual loner at worst.

Deciding against poking his head into his office to offer a sentiment of departure, Williams left the building, thankful that despite the abuse he would get when he got home at least he had his wife and kids there. He didn't want to contemplate the notion of arriving home to an empty house, a microwave meal and the endless banality that was evening television.

Chapter 5

The kitchen was filled with the smell of freshly cooked pasta, pesto and grilled chicken as Natalie sat at the small kitchen table, her father sitting silent across from her. As she pushed the food around her plate she glanced across at her father. His pretence of completing *The Times* crossword was transparent and fooled no one. She had seen her father like this many times before, most recently after the death of his wife, Natalie's mother, Mary. He wore the same look of fleeting interest as he moved the nib of the pen over clue after clue. His face bore the traces of concern etched into every laughter line and crevice.

'How you getting on?' she offered without meeting his eyes.

'Difficult one today,' he replied, absently.

'Unlike you, you normally have them finished before you bemoan the fact that a simpleton could have completed it.' She pushed the plate of half eaten food aside. 'Something on your mind you want to talk about?' George Soderman didn't reply quickly, but he did look up to meet his daughter's eyes. Finally, when he spoke, his voice was small, fragile sounding. In that instant Natalie saw a terrifying truth that she had kept hidden from herself. Her father was getting older, was looking older, and the ultimate realisation, that he would not be around for ever. The notion caught her off guard as if the idea was alien to her, as though she had never thought of it before.

'Just worried about you,' he replied as he got up from his chair and paced the small kitchen. 'What with the break-in at your place and those phone calls recently, just makes me worry that's all.'

'Look Dad, I'm sure it was just bored kids, at least I wasn't there when it happened.'

'I suppose we can be thankful for small mercies at any rate.'

'What's really the matter Dad, you look as though you have the weight of the world on your shoulders.'

'Aside from my baby daughter…'

'Dad, I'm thirty-three.'

'Don't interrupt,' he said with a smile, returning to sit opposite her. 'Being three or thirty-three makes no difference, you will always be my little girl and I will always worry about you despite what you say.' Natalie took a moment to get up from her seat and take her plate across to the kitchen counter. Leaning against the counter she looked out through the windows into the darkness the night offered.

Her father's cottage was one of five properties off the main street in Redburn. The Soderman residence was a Grade II listed timber framed cottage built in the sixteenth century, it was also the last house on the right; everything beyond was woods and fields as far as the eye could see. When she had been growing up she had loved the adventure that the woods and fields had brought with it, an exciting playground for a youthful mind. But now, returning much older and wiser, the darkness of the woods and the endless expanse of fields gave her tight knots of unease inside. It was as if every nightmare or horror film she had ever seen was within the boundary of the woods. Inwardly she cursed herself for too many late night Stephen King film fests, not to mention reading his books which she happened to think were much scarier than any of the film adaptations.

Despite his age, George Soderman was light on his feet. As he put his hands to his daughter's shoulders she jumped, her heart racing, lost in tangled thoughts of Pennywise the clown hunting her through the woods.

'Sorry, didn't mean to…' Natalie collapsed into her father's arms. 'Let's get you up to bed hey, it's been a long day, a good night's sleep will do you the world of good.' With that he led his daughter from the kitchen, out into the hallway and towards the stairs.

Pausing at the base of the stairs he thought he heard a movement outside the front door.

He waited, listening, but heard nothing more. Cursing himself for acting like a frightened child, he guided his daughter towards her bedroom hoping that his suggestion of a good night's sleep really would do the trick, but somehow believing none of the advice he had prescribed.

* * *

George sat on his daughter's bed, Natalie tucked beneath the white cotton covers. The room was warm, the curtains pulled across to shut out the night whilst the small bedside table lamp cast a welcoming glow.

'What are your plans for tomorrow?' he asked, trying to keep his voice as vague as possible but failing to do so.

'Nothing planned yet, but I suppose I will have to get onto the insurance company and speak to the police again as well, why?'

'No reason, I have to go into town tomorrow, wondered if you fancied meeting for a coffee.'

'I'd like that.'

Biting his lip, Natalie's father fought against the urge to say what he really wanted to say. As he stared across at his daughter he felt the years melt away, suddenly she was a young girl once again. The times he had sat where he was now when she had been unwell, a cold or chicken pox or sheer exhaustion, he had always sat here and made sure she was okay. He recalled all the worries he had had, probably still did have in one way shape or form. About her falling in with the wrong crowd, not studying hard enough, discovering drink and drugs, sneaking out at night, all of which went unfounded. But now, meeting the right guy, keeping safe in a world gone mad. Okay so she hadn't been a saint, and they had had their fair share of arguments but essentially she had been a good girl growing up. He was not so naive as to think that his daughter had been an angel, that she had not offered the occasional lie to cover for some kind of adventure, but all in all he couldn't complain. She had grown into a competent, beautiful and intelligent woman. He was proud of her, always had been, and always would be.

Leaning forward to plant a kiss on the middle of her forehead, George switched off the bedside lamp and made his way carefully from the room back downstairs to the study. He had heard the phone ring earlier in the evening; the answer phone had kicked in and taken the message. He knew who the caller had been but hadn't wanted to listen to the message whilst Natalie was within earshot.

Sitting at his desk, tiredness beginning to pull at his eyelids, the phone rang again.

The shrilling sound surprised him and he snatched up the phone with a stammer.

No one spoke on the other end of the phone but there was someone there, he knew it.

In the background he could just make out the tiny fragment of chatter, was it bar chatter, music, or perhaps a television?

'Hello.' He said again, trying to assert a measure of bravado that he didn't feel and that was certainly not there.

Then the voice spoke and ice ran through his veins.

'Have you told her yet?' the voice said, genderless, monotone but menacing. 'Guess you've seen the article in the local paper, shame about the homeless man, wasn't it George, but then again I bet you think he deserved it.' The question was a rhetorical one. 'Nice to see your daughter is home for a few days, bad luck about her flat getting broken into wasn't it?'

George slammed the phone down, anger seething, his knuckles white with rage.

The phone rang again and he immediately snatched the cradle in answer, a volley of words ready to spill but he checked himself, not wanting to wake Natalie and alert her to the call.

'Remember the countdown, one down, two to go.'

The phone went dead.

George Soderman remained with the handset in his hand for a few moments; his mouth arced in a silent scream. Finally he dropped the handset back into the cradle and sat back in his chair. His body was flushed with ice cold fear, his mind was a haze of confusion and his heart was beating hard and fast within his chest.

He clasped a hand to his chest, massaging it as the pain flared, making him wince.

His greatest fear was ever closer to realisation.

A voice in the back of his mind repeated its cry to go to the police, to tell them all that had happened. To add in the burglary and the phone calls that his daughter had received. But as always he stopped the idea short. He didn't want to involve the police. If he did, what else would be dragged up, the last thing he needed, the last thing he wanted, was for this to destroy everything he and his late wife had built up.

He just hoped that Harry Stone could help before it was too late.

Chapter 6

Maggie Dean pulled her blonde hair into a ponytail as she padded through the apartment, pausing only to collect the empty glass from the side of the bed. She left David asleep and exhausted in bed. She sniffed the glass and could only detect the strong odour of Jack Daniels; he hadn't noticed the large dose of Flunitrazepam that she had ground down into a powder before dropping it into his drink, by that stage he had been too wasted as it were. The drug, more commonly identified as Rohypnol, would help with its memory dulling effect. It would also give her enough time to disappear from David's life. Last night on the way home he had spoken of spending the day together, a notion she had not totally dismissed. Although in the back of her mind she knew what the next day would envisage, and it did not include David.

Pulling on her tee shirt and underwear she searched for the rest of her clothes.

It was time to leave.

By now her message would have been delivered to its recipient.

Things were progressing as she had planned, aside from the inclusion of the private investigator George Soderman had enlisted to find her, but that was okay, that was all part of the game, it made it all the more fun. Besides, no one had any recent pictures of her and she prided herself on her chameleon-like transformations, shedding a new identity as quickly as a person throws their exercise kit into the washing basket after a good run.

The thought of a run struck Maggie.

She hadn't been running for a few days now. She missed the freedom that it gave her, and loved nothing better than to find a spot that would offer both sanctuary and challenging terrain. Resolving to find time to go running later that day in amongst the turmoil and chaos that was her life, Maggie turned her thoughts back to the private investigator. He was an unknown quantity and one that would have to be watched carefully, although nothing and no one would detract from her plan.

Wondering if maybe it would be an idea to ask her ponytailed tattoo man to pay him a visit, Maggie entered the kitchen and washed out the glass before returning it to the cupboard, then she wiped down the surfaces of the kitchen before pulling on the rest of her clothes and slipping out of the apartment and into the early hours of a new day, a new day that promised her so much.

A smile creased her lips as she recalled a line from one of the Lethal Weapon films. "I'm mayhem and he's chaos". She couldn't recall which one of the male leads had said the line or indeed if it was the correct line spoken, besides which it was immaterial, the sentiment was right and it summed up her plan to a tee. What was about to happen was pure mayhem *and* chaos, or at least for Natalie Soderman and her father it would be.

Stifling a laugh, Maggie found herself buoyed by the knowledge that by the end of next week her vendetta would be complete, a grudge harboured for a long, long time would be all but debarred. She thought of all those hours sitting in solitary confinement, all those hours sitting with those therapists who tried to understand and dissect her, who tried to pull her apart in the name of "understanding". She thought of one of the therapists who had been almost brutal in his persistence to get inside her mind. What was his name? Foster or Faymoor…Fox…that was it, Dr Robert Fox.

Fox had been the only therapist who had heard the real Maggie Dean speak. All the others had been played, had been told what they wanted to hear, but Dr Fox got the picture. She had told him exactly what was inside her mind, what she wanted to do.

Maggie smiled.

Of course Robert Fox was a long time dead now, shame really, he had seemed nice enough.

The plan had been in her mind for as long as she could remember, it had all just been a matter of planning, of patience and waiting and then re-planning.

The time had come.

And for Natalie Soderman, her life expectancy was in freefall.

Chapter 7

Harry woke up on the sofa with the morning chill of a new day biting at his bones. His neck ached and no amount of rubbing did anything to ease the dull pain that would last for the duration of the day, he knew that from past experience.

Swinging his legs over the edge of the sofa, he realised that once again he had fallen asleep dressed in yesterday's clothes and with the television showing reruns of old BBC comedies he had first seen in his teens. He noticed that the familiar brown document wallet lay on the floor with the scattered contents of a lifetime's exploration with little to show by way of results.

He made his way strategically from a lounge that was littered with unpacked boxes and through to the kitchen, filled the kettle and set aside a mug for coffee. In the back of his mind he heard a nagging voice asking him why he hadn't yet unpacked the boxes from when he moved in some seven months ago.

The answer was a simple one.

The place still didn't feel like home.

Each time he returned through the front door he felt a sigh building from within and a heaviness surrounding his heart. The place felt cold, yet the heating was on. It was quiet, despite the music or the television.

The simple fact was that it just didn't feel like home, and he wondered if it ever would.

The oak framed cottage was set back from the main thoroughfare in the small village of Ravenswood St Thomas some twenty miles outside of the city centre. The cottage was a new build, only five years old in fact. After his mother had passed away in the middle of 2009, Harry had inherited a lump sum from the sale of a guest house she had run on the south coast. He had used part of the inheritance to purchase a self-build that had run out of money, steam and enthusiasm. He had bought the place and had it finished, but something, as yet unknown, still didn't make the cottage feel like home, his home. Perhaps it was the historical aspect of the place, maybe if he was a spiritual person he might think that the land the cottage was built on was tainted in some way. He knew that the previous cottage to stand on the land had burnt down some fifteen years ago and any properties that followed had all met with disaster after disaster, from leaking pipes to rotting timbers. He wondered if those strange occurrences would follow now that he was here.

The cottage was a four bedroom detached property, much larger than he needed, especially considering his current lack of romantic entanglements. But he liked the village with its small number of residents and coupled with his hatred of perpetual moving – something he had done a lot of in his twenties – he hoped to remain here for some time to come, barring any problems of course.

Whilst the kettle boiled Harry lethargically climbed the stairs with the notion of taking a shower, sleep still a visitor in his body from which it was proving hard to evict.

His mind was still feeling the groggy, almost drunken effects, of having met Sara yesterday evening. All he hoped was that the lamenting period would be quicker to clear this time.

* * *

Showered, shaved and in fresh clothes, Harry checked the time. He groaned when he saw that it was only just after six in the morning. He really wished he could sleep better but these days he seemed to survive on only a few hours before his mind was awake with his body following slowly in its wake.

Taking the coffee and a slice of toast back into the lounge, he gathered up the pile of papers and began sorting through them, hoping for inspiration to descend. It didn't.

His sister Charlotte had been missing for nearly seventeen years now, she would be thirty-four in two months time. He blocked out the *other* thought that was itching to be let loose, that monster of subtlety that was currently behind the proverbial caged door.

He was sure she was still alive, or at least that was what he kept telling himself. It was the entire reason he had become a private investigator who specialised in finding missing persons. The only irony was that nine times out of ten he could find his clients' missing but not when it came to his own investigation. That seemed to hit brick wall after brick wall.

Placing all the paperwork back into the folder he took it through to the room in the house that would, one day he had assured himself, become his study. At present it was a small box room on the ground floor with a desk and yet more boxes. There was a laptop that was still boxed, another present to himself from his late Mother's payroll. Another promise he had made himself was that one day he would sit down and remove it from its boxed home and actually use it in anger.

Half an hour later, having finished his coffee and breakfast, Harry Stone was sitting at his desk in his office in town. He was, as was the norm, on his own. From the corner of his desk his docked iPod played tracks that were shuffled and which, every now and again, caused him to look at the small grey unit and smile at the ease in which it mixed an eclectic playlist. The soul of Nina Simone competed with the acoustic folk-rock of Neil Young before giving way to the melodic contemporary adult rock that was Coldplay. Deciding that his current state of mind was in no way conducive to a Coldplay ballad, Harry pressed the forward button and relaxed when Simon & Garfunkel began singing about Mrs Robinson.

He stared at his two screens, one screen showed his emails whilst the dual monitor showed the database with the list of current matters and their status.

His mind was torn.

He really needed to speak with George Soderman about his

current employ; he was having no joy in tracking down Maggie Dean. It was as though she had simply vanished, which to all intents and purposes was what Soderman was hoping had happened to her, or worse. Either way all of his enquiries had returned a big fat zero. It was a similar story with Maggie Dean's father, Henry Glover. Since his release from prison and the break up of his marriage he had simply disappeared from sight.

Harry had had more luck tracing Maggie's mother, Angela Glover. She had been easier to locate, the only downside was actually trying to catch her when she was in. Despite numerous phone calls and messages left she had so far neglected to return a single message which left Harry with only a singular option, and one that he really didn't want to have to do, a face to face visit.

Deciding that he could no longer put off going through his email inbox, Harry began bulk deleting the junk and then started on what looked to him to be work-related mail.

One of the cases he was currently engaged in, a missing boy of sixteen had hardly moved in the last few months. After a burst of sightings and possible last known locations the trail had gone cold, the job had died on its feet, run out of steam and was close to being shelved. James Creswell was still missing and his parents still spending every last penny they had, and probably funds they didn't trying to find him.

Harry opened one of the messages from a contact in London who was helping him out on the Creswell case. Even before he saw the text he knew roughly what it would say.

But he was wrong.

He re-read the message three times before a smile creased his lips. Creswell had been found, or at least sighted in a semi-permanent place. He had been seen in Greek Street and Harry knew from friends that the place led from Soho through to Shaftesbury Avenue, one of the sightings that had died a death a month ago. Creswell had been seen in one of the restaurants there but his contact didn't say whether it was as a customer or as an employee. All that was certain was that James Creswell was alive and had been seen, and with that there meant there was still an element of hope.

Quickly flicking through his diary he decided that there was no time like the present so clicked on Internet Explorer and loaded the website to check the train times - the idea of driving to the capital doing nothing except accelerate a nagging discourse inside his head. Harry arranged a free time slot from the office diary and quickly typed his assistant a note, forwarding a copy of the email for reference.

Seeing as he had half an hour prior to the train's departure and having the luxury of being only five minutes from the station, Harry quickly went through the rest of his unread mail.

The final email was an enquiry. Normally he left these for his assistant Val to look over but seeing as he had enough time he had decided to act on the message himself.

The content of the email was no different from a lot of enquiries that his firm dealt with. The prospective female client wanted to meet to discuss services and fees regarding surveillance for a philandering husband. The client would be in town all day today and tomorrow and wondered if it was possible to meet later that day.

Never one to shun the lure of new clients and of course their fees, Harry forwarded the email to his assistant and asked her to invite the lady in later that day. Val would be able to get the case, if taken, up and running. He knew his assistant would be able to take care of the initial meeting, get all the required information and to open the electronic file.

Switching to his database program, Harry printed off the details for James Creswell, briefly flirting with the idea of trying to pay a visit to Angela Glover who resided in Southampton, wondering if maybe he would drop by on the way back, but deciding against it. He would do that tomorrow via car instead of train. He quickly entered the name of Margaret Mayhew, the prospective new client, into the system. His mind then returned to Maggie Dean and her whereabouts.

He just wished he knew where to find her, or at the very least, how to find her.

Chapter 8

Angela Glover rolled out of bed without subtlety or class. Stumbling through her bedroom that had the look of a room that had recently been ransacked by looters, she entered the bathroom, lent over the side of the bath and emptied the contents of her stomach. Her stomach hurt, her head ached and her insides felt as though they were trying to burst free not to mention the stinging pain between her legs.

Unsteady on her feet she peered through the bathroom door and noticed the pale buttocks of last night's patron who was still face down and comatose in her bed. Collapsing back into the bathroom she sat down on the toilet seat and caught sight of herself in the adjacent mirror. Her face was deathly pale, eyes wide and covered in the filmy glaze of a lifetime drunk. Her naked body, once slender and fresh, was now weighty and pasty-white. Varicose veins lined her bulk like a fanatically drawn roadmap that mingled with the bruises and scars of a life harshly lived.

She checked her neck and chest and found that it was littered with bite marks and scratches whilst her left eye was showing signs of a fresh blow.

Trying to fight the new wave of nausea that was threatening to spill, Angela crossed the bathroom to the sink and ran the cold tap before splashing water over her face. Despite her lack of recollection from last night's after hours endeavours she guessed that it had followed her pattern of normality that was her life.

She had started work in the bar in the early afternoon, by early evening she had already been feeling the effects of too many drinks – her tipple being scotch and soda - that had been bought for her. By the time last orders had been called she was already fair game for the foreign businessman who had been giving her the eye and plying her with drinks all evening.

He had been nice at first, gentlemanly in many ways, until she had said no to an intimate act that she had never even let her husband perform. Then he had turned nasty, the fists had been flying as were his venomous words, calling her a dirty prick tease and a whore. The words didn't affect her, she had been called a lot worse over the years when she had been growing up on the estate in Leeds, but the punches, they caught her off guard and from that she never recovered. After that she had been fair game for the brutality that followed, putting up a fight was never an option.

Wiping a grimy towel across her face, Angela heard movement from the other room. She quickly crossed the bathroom and shut the door, sliding across the bolt that she had fitted after a previous one night stand had tried his best to kick the door down in an attempt to reach her.

As she waited for the businessman to leave Angela considered her life, past and present. She thought about Henry for the first time in a long time, and thoughts of Henry made her think of Maggie and the other one. Maggie, she knew, had been sent to foster home after foster home after it became clear to the authorities that Angela Glover could not cope with the perils of bringing up a daughter. Besides, she had been pregnant with her second child when Henry had been sent to prison for his part in a burglary, although she knew he should have been going to prison for something much more shocking. She remembered it all as though it had been yesterday, such was the clarity of the memory. How could she forget the day her life simply ceased to exist in any meaningful way? Since that day she had been living in a world of pain that had never lessened, it had simply accelerated.

And then she had had her second child.

The one she had run away from, the one she had had to give away.

The one she had left to the mercy of the hospital.

As she sat on the toilet seat tears began to stain her cheeks and blur her already hazy vision.

It was the kindest thing to do for the child, what sort of life would she have given him or her. Having a father who was a convicted criminal and a sister who was showing an alarming leaning towards the same tendencies as her father, the same look in her eyes, dark and vacant yet somehow alarming all the same. It was surely not a good start for her child. It was probably the smartest thing she had ever done.

Wiping her eyes, Angela listened at the door until she was sure her visitor had gone before exiting the bathroom.

Returning to the room that carried the stench of stale sweat and sex, alcohol and sour cigarette smoke, she looked around her tiny bedsit and wondered if today would be any different from any other day? With a sigh she took a shower, the water stinging her skin in wave after wave of hurt. When finally she stepped from the shower and dried her aching bones, she dressed her wounds, knowing that she had to be back at the bar in a few hours to start all over again. She applied make-up more heavily around the bruised eye, doing her best to cover the blemish.

Perhaps I won't have a drink today; she said laughing to herself, knowing that failure was not so much of a possibility, more of a certainty.

Before closing the bathroom door she looked to the side of the bed where last night's company had left a pile of money as her reward. Something inside of her shrivelled and died, perhaps it was her dignity or her pride, or perhaps it was just the stark realisation of what her life had become.

Again she thought of both her children, her daughter Maggie and the child she didn't know. And again she wondered, hoped that their lives had worked out better than her own.

Chapter 9

When Natalie Soderman made her way slowly down the stairs at around 9:30 the next morning, the smell of fresh coffee and toast uncovered a painted canvas of long since forgotten memories. She paused at the bottom of the stairs and listened to the sounds of the house, the ticking of the hallway clock, the gentle sound of the radio coming from her father's study. With silent feet she made her way towards the doorway and stood leaning against the frame. Her father sat in his chair with a folder open on his knees. He was flicking through page after page and despite the angle she could make out the mixture of black and white and coloured images. She watched as he ran a hand across his forehead, pausing to massage the creases at the top of his nose, it was something he had always done, a sign of stress, that something was seriously bothering him.

From the hallway the telephone began ringing.

Natalie shrank back away from the door, listening as her father got up from his chair and padded down the hallway to answer the call. In his hands he clutched the folder.

'Hi…yes it's fine to talk…okay…look why don't I come to you… yes okay that works for me…no, no that's fine, I'll make sure that Natalie is nowhere close…okay…' after a few moments George Soderman replaced the handset and stood there looking at the telephone as though he had never seen one before, as though it was the most alien of devices to him before returning to his study.

Natalie retraced her steps to the base of the stairs and quickly entered the kitchen where she opened a cupboard and took out a cup, rattling it against another, signalling her arrival, doing her best to show that she had heard nothing of his call. Sure enough, a few seconds later, her father appeared at the door. His face looked flushed and she could see he was fighting the urge to rub the centre of his forehead.

'Morning,' she said, matter-of-factly. 'Fancy a cuppa?'

'Morning sweetheart,' he said, crossing the kitchen and placing a gentle kiss on her cheek. 'Sleep well?'

'Better than I thought I would, what about you?'

'You know me, sleep through a thunderstorm I would.' Natalie didn't say anything but she knew a lie when she heard one. She let it go and returned her efforts to making the tea.

'What you up to today?'

'Want to pop into town to grab a few bits, I don't normally cater for very adventurous food, and seeing as I have a guest I had better get some in, I also have a couple of jobs I want to do.'

'Anything I can do or help with?'

'You just take it easy, get some rest.'

'Why don't I meet you in town, go for a coffee or something?'

'Do you mind if we take a rain check, if I can get all my jobs done today then perhaps tomorrow we can meet up, what do you say?'

'Of course, tomorrow is fine and besides I can then try and get you to try one of those disgustingly bad cakes they serve as well,' she said with a playful smile. 'Perhaps I'll take a stroll in the village instead, have a wander around the woods, and there's the book shop I want to pop into.'

'Good, good.' He replied absently, his mind already elsewhere.

* * *

Natalie sat with her coffee on the sofa in the lounge. Her father had already lit the fire in an effort to banish the chill from a day that was grey, overcast and held the promise of more of the same. She looked around the lounge, realising how little it had changed over the years. It was a room of simple taste and design, yet it held memories aplenty.

The two long beige sofas sat opposite one another and flanked both sides of the large inglenook. Between the sofas stood a low table with an ornate tray that doubled as one large coaster, whilst next to that were several magazines piled in a neat fashion; a cook book that had seen better days, a historical account of ancient Britain and a television guide.

Natalie thought of her mother Mary. She missed her so much, the loss still fresh despite the years. Not wanting to lose herself to a flood of tears that were threatening to spill, Natalie thought of her father again. She thought of the telephone call she had overheard, the almost clandestine nature of it. Then there was the look of him, the haunted, almost haggard look he was carrying around. Something was clearly troubling him but she knew it was pointless to ask, he simply wouldn't say, he would keep it hidden until he was ready to tell. Much like herself, she admitted with a sly smile.

In that instant she decided what she was going to do. Once he had gone out later in the day she was going to break one of her father's few house rules, she was going to snoop in his study; she had to find the truth about what was going on with him, to find out what he was not telling her. Besides which, the snooping would keep the memories of yesterday's horror away for a short while. At least that was the hope.

* * *

George Soderman had returned to the study with his cup of coffee and the weight of so much pressing down upon his shoulders. In the kitchen he had been so close, so very, very, close to telling his daughter everything. She knew about being adopted, that was something they had not hidden from her, but likewise it had never been a problem, just a mere point in a past that they, and more importantly Natalie, had moved on from. It was something that had always impressed both Mary and himself, the mature way in which Natalie had accepted the nature of her past, and at the same time not asked to delve into that dark void to learn the true nature of her blood parents and the reasons for her adoption.

He had wanted to tell her about the phone calls, the threats, the fact that he knew the burglary at her flat were all symptoms of the same disease, and that disease was her past that was doing everything in its power to catch up with her.

After speaking with Harry Stone he had agreed to meet him later in the day when the investigator had returned from a job he was doing in London. Stone was going to ring when he was on his way back, and arrange to meet at the investigator's office to be sure that Natalie could not overhear any of what they needed to speak about.

His mind though was made up, this evening, after he returned from seeing Stone, he was going to sit his daughter down and confess all. She had a right to know the truth, it affected her too.

He had to.

For her own sake.

Chapter 10

Maggie Dean shut the door to the office of Hunter Stone and Co. with a smile etched across her features. She had met with Stone's assistant, a petite woman of advanced years and grey hair who had been cordial, professional and pleasant but with a hint of mistrust. Maggie thought she had played her part well, had given nothing away, but the old woman gave off a different impression. Or maybe that was just her nature. Either way Maggie believed that she had outwitted the woman for the purpose of her need.

She had provided paperwork to verify who she was, or at least who her cover was. Her fake papers were as good as ever. They had cost her, but they had never let her down.

She had been in the office no more than a quarter of an hour, enough time to deliver her planned story, her bogus tale of a husband having an affair. The name of the man and his location were in London and by the time they realised that he was not married to any Margaret Mayhew it would all be over.

Maggie had taken in as much of the layout of the offices as possible; she would talk to Drake and ask him to pay an after dark visit, or maybe she would do it, she would have to see how things were going. She wanted to find out as much as possible about the investigator and the information he was working with, what information he had on her, how far he was getting, how close he was getting.

It was as she began heading for her car that her phone beeped signifying the arrival of a new message.

The message was from Drake. He had arrived at his location. She smiled to herself.

Once Natalie had been taken care of she would have to deal with Drake. He simply knew too much to live. But not yet; before that there were other things to be taken care of.

Chapter 11

The barmaid handed over the change and pushed the two pints of Guinness across the bar to two grizzled looking men who leered drunkenly in her vague direction before swapping lurid comments and moving over to one of the booths along the side of the bar.

Angela smiled to herself; it was nothing new to her, more a case of par for the course. Water off a duck's back as her mother would have said. What was it that she had once read, was it a line from a book that expressed perfectly her sentiments? Same shit different day wasn't it? And here it was no different, same men different day. Her thoughts were interrupted as a tall man pushed open the entrance to the bar and shuffled his way towards her. His head was covered by the hood of his sweatshirt whilst his face was silhouetted by the dimness of the lighting.

As he reached the bar he pulled up a chair, almost slumping, without removing his head gear.

'What can I get you?' Angela asked.

'Cider, pint of.' The newcomer grunted in reply as he dug some change from his pocket and left it spilled over the counter. With pint in hand the man crossed to the booth by the door and sat facing the bar. A day old crumpled edition of a tabloid newspaper lay on the table which the man absently flicked through, pausing momentarily on each page as if digesting a portion of the news before moving on to the next. Reading but not reading what his eyes were seeing. Every now and again he would look up at the bar, keeping an eye on the aged barmaid who pottered about her business, collecting glasses and wiping down the counter.

He had found his target.

* * *

Robbie Drake was tired and frustrated, even more so as he was unhappy with his current assignment. He didn't have a problem sitting in a bar drinking cider from a kitty that was not his own. He didn't even mind flicking through a day old newspaper in search of any article, celebrity or otherwise, that interested him and if he was honest not a lot did. As far as he was concerned the best thing for the mass of so called reality stars and celebrity nobodies, was death by any means painful. He turned over the page which had a full colour story about some ex-singing celebrity who was now sober and clean again after her seventh trip to rehab. Drake wondered how long it would be before her next book and television series tie in was up and running - either that or she would end up dead.

What Drake was unhappy about was the fact that he had had to drive up to London, a journey he hated, and deal with some mature bar crone who thought she was still in her twenties but was anything but.

Maggie had been explicit in her instructions.

He had to deal with the husband and former wife that were Henry and Angela Glover.

She would deal with her sister personally.

His directives were plain and simple, keep an eye on her and at the first opportunity, despatch his own brand of brutality.

Finishing his pint of cider Drake returned to the bar and ordered another one, this time he removed his hood and engaged in conversation with the woman.

* * *

Angela busied herself with putting away some of the glasses she had just run through the cleaner. Every now and again her eyes caught sight of the tattooed man in the booth by the door. Despite his initial frostiness in temperament and manner she warmed to him when he spoke. His voice was like velvet and his eyes were dark pools full of unknown mystery. He was handsome in a kind of rough and ready way.

After he had ordered his third pint they were both freely speaking, so much so that he moved from his booth to the bar, leaving the pages of celebrity and their lives of nonsense behind.

She caught his glances, furtive yet probing.

Every round he bought he offered her a drink which she happily accepted. Her first shift finished mid-afternoon and she had a good idea what she would be doing between shifts.

The two men with the leering glances and lurid comments left the bar leaving Angela and the tattooed man alone. Afternoons were mostly slow, sometimes with only herself as company for a little while. Most people who stumbled in were lifetime drunks or those who were lost and either in need of liquid refreshment or who had wandered into the wrong place.

'Just me and you then.' He said, suggestive with a hint of playfulness.

'Well aren't you the lucky one.' She replied with a wink. Robbie Drake returned the smile, knowing that her luck was about to run out.

Chapter 12

Harry Stone did not have far to wander from his office until he found a smattering of pubs, coffee houses, supermarkets, and book and knick-knack shops, all of which aided him when the urge to wander took grip. But when a case was pressing on his mind and he needed to think things through, to get a little space, to lose himself for a while, he would grab himself a coffee from Starbucks or Café Nero, depending on the queues and make his way to the park across town. It was a quick walk from the train station, on one side of the road fields and wide open space, whilst opposite was a row of elegant looking houses. And it was here that Harry found himself wandering now, a place of solace, as though returning into the arms of a loved one.

Simply called *The Gardens*, Harry found himself meandering through the expanse of green that was linked by small rustic bridges over low rivulets of water. Here the rivers were not littered with the discarded shopping trolleys and leftover clutter that was evident in the main city centre rivers. You could hear the playful cries of the young as tired parents tried to expend as much energy from their offspring as possible within the confines of a fenced play area, whilst swans and ducks inhabited the rivers and roamed the grassy vicinity. In the distance small specks of white could be seen in far off fields, the sheep luxuriating in their large expanse of grazing ground.

It was here in the gardens that he had donated a mahogany tinted bench with a rectangle plaque which read "*To a good friend who is greatly missed – Laurence Hunter 1934 – 2009*".

The bench was multi-layered with sentiments. He had placed the bench with the plaque here because Hunter had been his mentor, as well as friend and confidant but he was also the man who had left the firm to Harry, who had given him purpose and a profession, not to mention a future. The bench was where he also came to think about everything else, about his mother who had died in the same year as Hunter, a mother who he had been close to in childhood but whose relationship had faltered and ultimately disintegrated in her final years, something that he regretted but was now unable to rectify. He thought of his sister Charlotte who was still missing, presumed dead, but who he hoped above anything else, was still out there some place, alive and well, just waiting to be found. Finally, about his father who, despite speaking to him only occasionally and seeing him even less, he loved and dreaded the day when he wasn't there.

As Harry sat, gazing out lost in thought, his mind returned to the Creswell case. The case would soon be marked as closed. His visit to London had not been wasted. The outcome should have pleased him, another job completed, another missing soul found alive and well, another bill to be paid but that wasn't the case. There would be no happy reunion for Mr and Mrs Creswell who had engaged his services. James Creswell had been found, but by now he would be long gone. His desire not to be found was only equalled in his desire not to return to his family home, to the parents who, despite a public facing show of grief and loss were in truth controlling, manipulative and did little to let him live his own life.

Thoughts of the Creswell's were superseded by that of Maggie Dean.

A sudden thought flashed across his mind.

Why did Maggie Dean want to remain hidden? George Soderman had employed him to locate Maggie, her mother Angela and father Henry. So far he had only located Angela. Henry, like his daughter, seemed to have vanished off the face of the earth. Ever since his stint in prison he had been off the radar, a nomad, wanting to and managing successfully to avoid detection in the system that was everyday life. No bank accounts, no home address or mobile, nothing that tied him to any place. He was quite simply a ghost walking the streets. Maggie Dean on the other hand, what was her rationale? Soderman was keeping something from him, that much was evident by his evasiveness at certain questions, perhaps now it was time to get to the truth.

He had spoken to the man this morning having rung him on his journey to London. He had arranged to see him later this afternoon, a meeting that would be his next action of the day and his strategy was a simple one, the truth or a call to arms, case closed. Soderman could find himself another investigator.

For a precious few seconds Harry tried to empty his mind of all work and personal related thoughts and just looked in the direction of the gardens and the view of the Cathedral as its backdrop. It was stunningly beautiful and Harry couldn't help but be amazed by its sheer size, relevance in history and the city and the visitors who streamed through its doors daily.

* * *

'So what is it you're not telling me George?' Harry asked as Val laid out the tray of coffee on the round table in what passed as the conference/meeting room. The older man shifted uneasily in his seat, his eyes looking anywhere but at Harry Stone. The investigator waited for a response and busied himself with pouring the coffee. Finally his client spoke, albeit with eyes averted.

'I'll be honest with you Mr Stone.' The investigator did not interrupt the man to remind him that it was fine to call him by his christian name. 'I haven't been entirely truthful with you, and for good reason.'

Harry looked on impassively.

Outside he heard the sound of a car horn beeping as he waited for his client to speak. Finally George Soderman broke the silence.

'I engaged your services, initially, for one reason and one reason only, to locate three persons of the Glover family.'

'Correct.'

'That was entirely truthful, I did want to know where they currently were and for one very good reason.'

'Your step daughter Natalie...'

'My daughter Natalie.' Soderman cut in, emphasising the point in his usual tactful way. Harry knew that Soderman had been a lecturer before retiring and had a feeling that he had cut students dead with the same authoritive yet friendly manner all those years ago.

'Sorry, your daughter Natalie.'

'As you correctly say Natalie is not my blood daughter, but she has been with us – me – since she was only a matter of weeks old, to all intents and purposes she is as good as a blood daughter.'

'And what difference does finding these three people make to Natalie, apart from the fact that they are blood related?' Soderman clasped his case and pulled from it a copy of the local paper, he flicked through to the page with the news story of the homeless man found drowned in the river and passed it across to Stone.

'I read about this.'

'I think you'll find that that is the man you are looking for, Henry Glover.' Stone was about to offer sentiments of disbelief when Soderman passed across a picture of Glover that he had managed to get hold of showing a much younger Glover. It was the same man though. The eyes told enough.

'Death by misadventure, infighting amongst the homeless community?' Stone offered still reading from the article.

'Sources of mine say strangulation.'

'That's some serious infighting, murder you say?' Soderman said nothing but for the first time met the eyes of the investigator. 'And if it is murder you think this has something to do with Natalie and the other two?' A silence fell between the two men; Soderman took a sip of coffee whilst Stone returned the papers.

'I've had some phone calls at home.'

'From?'

'Can't say.'

'Male or female?'

'Again, hard to say, voice is disguised using one of those voice boxes. The number is always withheld when I try and redial.'

'What about going through your telephone company?'

'I did that; all numbers came back to dead lines.'

'What did the caller say?'

'Threats mainly.'

'To Natalie?'

'Yes. But then her house was broken into. Again maybe no connection but…'

'Coincidence.' Stone said, knowing that on this notion both men were agreed. 'Anything else?'

'The last call I had was yesterday evening.'

'Same voice?'

'Same disguised voice yes.'

'What did they say?'

'Asked if I had seen the local paper.'

'Relating to the homeless man article?'

'Precisely.'

'Did they say anything else?' Soderman paused, let his eyes shy away from the man across from him as if searching for any corner of the room.

'The voice said something about a countdown, one down two to go.'

'Exactly that?'

'Yes I think so.'

'Anything else?' Again George paused.

'The voice on the phone knew of Natalie being back home with me.' Harry mused for a moment whilst finishing his coffee

'And you're sure you are telling me everything? Not holding anything back?' Harry could tell from the way he averted his eyes and the look of unease that crept over his face that there was still something he was not spilling. The investigator stood up from his seat and paced the room.

'If you want me to help you George I am going to need the facts, no matter what they are. No matter what skeletons are in the family cupboard, no matter what your fears, you have to tell me everything otherwise I cannot help you. Now, for the last time, what are you not telling me?' Finally, after a pause that seemed to span ages, the older man spoke.

'Years ago I found out by accident more than design, that a student of mine from years ago was now a therapist and had been assigned Maggie Glover. He obviously couldn't tell me any of the specifics of the sessions of the girl, but he told me enough. She had been attending therapy after being released from the juvenile correction facility, something of a regular occurrence for her I understand.'

'Okay, the relevance?'

'There were rumours that in one of the sessions Maggie Glover, nee Dean, harboured shall we say disturbing notions of revenge against her family who disowned her and a sister who appeared to have a better life than she? In short, she had a vendetta list. The list contained names of those people who had upset her in some way, those very people who she wanted to avenge and retaliate against.'

'And you think her family were on that list?'

'I know they were on that list, right there sitting at the top.'

The words from the phone call now came back with a stark relevance. Both men looked at one another and exchanged worried frowns before the investigator spoke.

'Shit! One down, two to go.'

Chapter 13

The village of Redburn had hardly changed in the intervening years which had seen Natalie Soderman leave for university life and eventually set up home in London. On the odd weekend when she returned home with piles of unwashed clothes and a craving for sleep, the changes had gone pretty much unnoticed, until now. The odd row of new houses appeared here whilst a newsagent had closed there, replaced by a book shop, a betting shop or a One Stop mini-supermarket.

Having earlier visited Redburn Cemetery to lay some flowers on her mother's grave, the dark-haired woman with the pale features that stood on the edge of Main Street, looked lost in thought, as though she had been wandering and had only now opened her eyes and found out where she had ended up.

Natalie looked across the street with the cluster of trees, man-made lake, pavilion and children's play area that made up *The Green* behind her, she looked at the row of shops that was the main hub of the village.

It was as though she was that little girl again, the one who had played with her friends in the park and the surrounding woods from morning till evening. It was as though she was back living in a time long before the world had seemingly gone mad, before the world had tried to constrict children's childhood into an ever decreasing amount of years. When life appeared to be simple and free from danger. Of course that wasn't true, there were the Moors Murders in the 1960s, the disappearance of Suzy Lamplugh in the mid 1980s and the Bulger case of the early 1990s to testify to that, and many more besides. Back then there just weren't as many media agencies vying for top billing. The media monster as it is now was back then a mere blip on the future of mankind.

In amongst the memories came the reality. Her eyes fell upon The Redburn Arms public house where she had worked so many long shifts behind the bar, trying her hardest to earn her own money and save for something that had seemed important at the time but which now she could no longer recall.

The place needed painting and the windows were grimy and soiled, outside a sandwich board was advertising the next round of Premiership Football matches happening over the coming weekend, whilst next door stood a newly opened second hand shop.

As thoughts of her happy childhood seeped over one another like waves lapping gently on a sandy beach, Natalie thought about her father. Something was troubling him; she would stake her life on it, it just wasn't like him. Their family ethos had always been to share one another's problems and not to hold any issues they had inside.

After he had left earlier that afternoon she had entered his study but she had found nothing. The folder she had seen him looking through, the one that he had clutched whilst standing in the kitchen, was gone. He had either locked it away in his filing cabinet or taken it with him and there was nothing that could, or would, explain his anxious appearance.

Glancing down at her watch she noticed that it was nearly late afternoon. Her father would be on his way home soon and she wanted to be there when he got back. Whatever it was that was bothering him she wanted to know.

Taking a quick glance at the pub, making a mental note to pop in and have a drink later in the week, Natalie left the main thoroughfare of the village and strolled across the green grass of her childhood, pausing only to cross the road that merged Main Street with Woodland Road.

As she turned left and sauntered unhurriedly along Hayward Way towards home, Natalie failed to notice the woman with the blonde hair pulled back in a ponytail who was watching her from a parked car on the approach road to the retirement home. If she had taken a moment she would have noticed a startling resemblance to herself. As it was she merely continued on her merry way.

* * *

Surprised to find the front door unlocked, Natalie entered the house and heard the sound of Billie Holiday singing *That Old Devil Called Love* emitting from the stereo in the lounge. She smiled. Her father was not a person who owned a lot of CDs, let alone a man who bought many. The Billie Holiday CD that was playing now was one that she had bought him last Christmas. It was a compilation that she had found whilst sauntering through one of the local markets near to her home.

Removing her coat and dropping her set of keys on the hall table, Natalie entered the kitchen and found her father hard at work chopping onions ready to fry.

'Hey!' she said entering the kitchen.

'Hey yourself.' George Soderman replied, sipping from a glass of red wine without turning around to greet his daughter. Natalie couldn't recall her father ever taking a drink before his own self-imposed seven p.m. watershed.

A quick glance at the clock on the wall told her that it was only after five p.m., his own rule had most certainly been ignored today. A rule he had lived by for as long as she could remember, and not even in those dark days after the death of his wife did he waver in spite of his emotional state. 'Can I get you a glass of wine?' he asked, taking a glass from a shelf and pointing in the general direction of the open bottle of Rioja on the side.

'Thanks I think I will,' his daughter replied, taking the proffered glass and pouring a generous quantity. Both fell into a silence as the void was filled with the gentle voice of Billie Holiday as she ended one song and began singing another.

George Soderman was the first to put his glass down.

'Natalie?' His daughter turned to face him and her fears were confirmed. He hardly ever called her by her christian name, and normally it was when something serious had happened or when she had done something that he did not fully approve of.

The last time he had spoken her name like that had been on the night he had rung to tell her that her mother had died. From behind wide eyes that were brimming with tears, Natalie saw her father stiffen with unease.

'What is it?'

'Come and sit down, I want to talk to you about something.'

'Are you okay, what has happened?'

'Please, just come and sit down and let me talk.' Natalie took her glass of wine and sat at the table where only this morning she had shared breakfast with her father. As George Soderman joined her, bringing with him the now half full bottle of red, she could see that he was uneasy, jittery almost.

'Dad, you're scaring me, what is it?'

A moment of silence passed before the speech he had been rehearsing in his mind for the best part of thirty years began its journey to freedom. He parted his lips and spoke in a quiet, almost whispery voice

.

Chapter 14

The room was cold and quiet and lay cloaked in semi-darkness. The smell of damp mingled with the heady scent of overpowering perfume caught in his throat like a thick cloying fog as he fought the urge to gag. Angela Glover lay on the bed, she was naked and still, whilst he sat across the room in a high-backed reading chair that had seen better days.

He was naked.

His body was covered in goose bumps and raised hairs. His penis sat flaccid and spent between his legs and from the flat above he heard movement followed by the flushing of the toilet cistern.

He felt both infuriated yet contented.

From the dim street light that broke through the split in the curtains, Drake let his eyes roam around the dilapidated room. He knew he should send a message to Maggie but couldn't be bothered to get up and find his jacket. He knew he should make tracks and quickly but again, he lacked the urgency and the motivation to do so.

From outside came the heavy artillery of drum and bass followed by the screeching of tyres and more beeping of horns. The neighbourhood appeared to resemble a war zone whose enemy factions were noisy neighbours and their counterparts in law enforcement. By all accounts he had stayed in some rough areas but this seemed to beat them all hands down.

Drake pushed his weary body from the chair; he had to gather his clothes and leave this place now, he had to go now or else...

Chapter 15

Maggie was growing impatient and annoyed as she sat in the car deciding if now really was the right time or perhaps she should wait a little longer. Her knuckles were white as she squeezed them into tight little balls, the frustration boiling rapidly. Taking one breath after another in an attempt to contain the rising anger, Maggie bit down on her lip, enough to break the skin and feel the coppery metallic taste of spilt blood.

When she had been growing up she had been in and out of juvenile institutions, one foster family after another. Always it was the same modus operandi. She wondered, fleetingly, if she had inherited her malevolence from her father or whether she was just a victim of circumstance and condition.

She checked her mobile phone and again found no messages waiting. *How long does it take?* She heard herself say. She had hoped that Drake would have been back by now, she had wanted him to pay a visit to the investigator's office and see if they could see what he had found out, rifle through the files, try and see what stage they were currently at. It was all about timing, and Maggie wanted to know how much time she had before either George or the investigator dragged in the police. Besides, she still had things she needed to sort out before things went that far. In the back of her mind she saw herself free when all this was over. Living some place else, free from the constraints that life had dealt her. But in reality, she saw a different outcome. Perhaps she had resigned herself to the inevitable truth of what would happen. Then again, she thought, in life you just never know, and she wanted to make sure that her Plan B was as ready as it could be, just in case.

Besides, at the moment Soderman had kept away from the police, not wanting to reveal his daughter's true bloodline to her, but he would have to soon enough. Fear and trepidation, or maybe on advice from the investigator, would push him down that path.

Pushing the car door open she stepped out into the dark evening deciding that if she hadn't heard from Drake by the time she had finished at the Soderman's then she would have to undertake that little job herself.

Instantly the chill of the breeze on her skin cooled and calmed her, it always did.

Maggie had driven past the turn off to the road she needed. She had parked the car in a clearing that was shrouded in darkness and offered no means of detection.

She knew where the house was, knew the best way into the property without being seen by prying and curious eyes.

When she had first discovered that she had a sister, Maggie had resolved to find her through any means possible. She wanted to know what her sister was like, where she was living, what her life was like. She had friends in low places and they came in handy when pressed hard enough. Before too long she had located the girl and the family who had adopted her.

Since then she had kept tabs on her, made frequent visits to the village of Redburn, and had even been inside the family home. It hadn't been difficult. Studying the family's comings and goings from afar she had soon located the spare key that the Sodermans foolishly left outside.

Once inside the house she had seen the proud pictures that adorned the walls and shelves, the three of them, one happy family. Maggie wasn't sure what grated her so much, what angered her so. The fact that she had a sister who appeared not to want to know anything about her family, that she had a loving home, or that she was jealous of the way her sister's life had turned out

Except of course their little oasis had soon dissipated when the mother had died. The perfect family were now down to two.

Digging a pocket torch from her jacket, Maggie trudged through the woods that backed onto the properties in Hayward Way; a smile was etched on her features, the excitement of what was to come.

After a few moments she found herself facing the back of the Soderman residence. The upper section of the house was in darkness, downstairs only a couple of lights were on, the curtains pulled against the night sky and the evils that lurked beyond.

Maggie took a set of keys from her pocket, a set that she had copied from an earlier visit to the house. Sometimes evil was a closer neighbour than anyone thought.

Chapter 16

Harry stood in the shower and let the jets of hot water spray over him, washing away the stress of the day. His mind was muddled and bemused. He had failed to find Henry Glover, yet the convicted felon had arrived in the form of a lifeless body hauled from a river. Maggie Dean was doing a universally fantastic impression of the invisible woman. And what annoyed him the most, was the one person he had located, Angela Glover, was now not answering her phone – cell or landline – and the bar she worked in had told him that she had not turned up for work this evening.

The case he had taken on for George Soderman had become more complex and had entered the realms of which he had never penetrated before. It was still, at its very core, a missing person's case, and like all missing person cases, the intended was doing their best to remain hidden. Maggie Dean was simply nowhere to be seen despite his extensive searching through most means possible.

Yet on the other hand the case was surely one for the police if Soderman was right in saying that Natalie and her father were in danger. If what Soderman had said was true, and if the homeless man found in the river was indeed Henry Glover then he was entering unchartered territory. He had an acquaintance who worked at Police Divisional Headquarters about five minutes drive from his office. His name was Tony Scott and he had met him some years before when he had just started working with Laurence Hunter. Back then the guy had been a detective constable, wet behind the ears and newly promoted from police constable. He was a man with a tenacious attitude at getting to the bottom of investigations and was known to have a temper when pushed too far the wrong way. In the back of his mind he felt sure that the man was now an inspector, although he was unsure if it was at the rank of DI or a DCI. Maybe he could give him a call and ask his advice.

What was more he was uneasy because he had been unable to contact Angela Glover. In the back of his mind he felt sure that a spectre of malevolence was lurking, ready to pounce when the time was right.

Feeling a chill creep over his exposed flesh, he turned off the shower and quickly wrapped a towel around his body. As he climbed out of the bath-cum-shower, Harry tried to recall where he had written Scott's number, hoping that it wasn't at the office. He also made a mental note to add the phone number, when found, into his mobile phone.

* * *

Having dressed in a pair of jogging bottoms and a sweatshirt, Harry returned downstairs and switched on the stereo, not liking the oppressive silence that appeared to be closing around him. Incapable of deciding on what music he felt like listening to, he finally took The Cure's greatest hits from a stack of CDs, inserted the disc into the machine, and then pressed play.

As Robert Smith pushed aside the silence and launched into *Boys Don't Cry*, Harry entered the kitchen and took a beer from the fridge. He didn't feel much like eating but needed to quieten the complaining growls emanating from his stomach. He checked the cupboards and the fridge for what constituted food of any description.

Finally deciding on an open tin of beans from the fridge and ignoring the spots of green that were growing on the crusts of the bread, Harry took the food to the kitchen table and ate without any desire to enjoy; it was simply a means to an end.

With the meal eaten, Harry felt a great weariness descend over him. He was dead on his feet, but knew what the scenario would be if he should climb the stairs to bed. The minute he laid his body down his mind would go into overdrive and sleep would be like a mirage in the Sahara; seemingly close but ultimately distant.

Deciding that going to bed was a waste of time and energy, Harry placed the tin of beans and the small plate on the side. He opened a cupboard and took out the half full bottle down from the shelf along with a glass. Pouring himself a small measure of Jim Beam he added two lumps of ice and returned to the kitchen table.

It was here he seemed to spend most of his time these days.

The room was warm and contained most of what he needed.

It also held the large kitchen table which he used to spread out files and case notes. Taking a sip of his drink he went through in his mind the list of cases that were in progress at present. Always wanting to be at the ready should something change that required his immediate attention.

The Creswell case was almost complete, if not for the parents then at least for him. The Sanders case was a missing person's enquiry going back some fifteen years, he was the fourth investigator to be employed to look into the matter and so far he had reached the exact point the previous three had reached, absolute zilch. He felt sure that it would only be a matter of time before his services were usurped and another firm was engaged and the whole process would begin again like some ridiculous version of Groundhog Day with only the investigator personnel changing.

The Robinson case was nearing a conclusion; an Asian family wanted their daughter's prospective husband investigated after concerns about income and associations with various left wing groups had been called into question. He had worked a similar case eighteen months back and it appeared that his name was respected among the Asian community.

Then of course there was the Soderman case, that was all very active and appeared to be moving ahead at a fast pace, maybe too fast. And finally there came the two new clients, the Mayhew case and the Jenkins case. The former, from the notes he had read of the meeting with his assistant, was a straightforward case of a philandering husband, another source of constant business revenue. It seemed cheating husbands were never as clever as they thought. Then again perhaps when the reverse happened husbands were more likely to take matters into their own hands instead of employing the services of an investigator to find out what was going on with their unfaithful wives. Harry hoped that he would have that one wrapped up soon enough. The latter was a case relating to the tracking down of several beneficiaries after the recent death in the family. Either way all the jobs paid the bills and, despite being in that middle ground of not poor but not rich, Harry Stone was thankful for the work.

His mind wondered once more if maybe it was time to employ a junior investigator, someone who could help out with the caseload. The firm was in a healthy enough position, considering the current economical hardship facing most corners of the world. Val had been on at him for some time now, always sending little email messages or commenting that a friend of a friend would be perfect for a junior job and so forth. The truth was, Harry had seriously thought about it. But with him it was like everything else he ever did, it just took time to make that elusive final decision.

Deciding to come back to the specifics of that conundrum another day, he drained the glass of the amber liquid whilst agreeing in principal that he would look into hiring someone before the middle of the year was reached.

Refilling the glass with another measure, Harry took the glass through to the lounge where the sound of The Cure was doing nothing to help his mood. He silenced the CD and sat down on one of the single sofa seats. He placed the glass on the side table and leant his head back against the chair.

Within a few minutes sleep took a firm grip.

The dark veil of sleep had descended down over his weary mind, but sleep would not last long before he would be disturbed.

Chapter 17

George Soderman returned to the kitchen table and sat alone.

He had opened his mouth to speak at the exact instant the police who were investigating the burglary had decided to call. Natalie sat there passively at first, but slowly and surely, the look of worry had appeared over her face. She made a gesture of apology and had taken the call out into the hallway and eventually upstairs to her bedroom.

Her father could not hear what was being said or gauge the reaction in words by his daughter, but it didn't sound promising. His mind returned to the phone call and the mention of the burglary, of Maggie Dean being behind this in one way or another. He wanted to say something, perhaps leave an anonymous tip with the police but what if that then brought them circling like vultures to his door. Would it be a bad thing?

Trying to suppress the cacophony of thoughts that were raging in his mind, all trying to drown one another out, he looked across at the diced onions that were still sitting on the chopping board, the can of unopened tomatoes still on the worktop and the pan he was going to make the bolognaise mixture in, empty and, he guessed, it would remain that way.

He had made his way to the study and retrieved the folder where he kept all of his notes and those that had been given to him by Harry Stone.

He had returned to the kitchen table with the folder when a noise out in the hallway dragged him from his thoughts.

He hadn't heard Natalie come down the stairs but found himself calling her name. When no answer came and with the hairs on the back of his neck rigid with the foreboding that something nasty was about to creep along his spine, Soderman got up from his chair and walked into the hallway.

She stood there bold as brass.

She looked different from the pictures he had been able to get hold of but it was her alright. If anything it was the eyes. They were the same vacant voids of emptiness that had looked up from the page of the newspaper the other day when the homeless man's picture had been printed.

The similarity to her father was unmistakable.

But what was even more startling was the similarity to Natalie. He hadn't really noticed it in the images he had of her from years back. But if her hair had been dark then…

George tried to push the look of surprise from his face but failed. He tried to find his voice but found it had deserted him for the time being.

'Hi George,' she said, dressed in black clothes and with her blonde hair tied back in a ponytail. Still he couldn't get the alarming notion out of his mind that if Natalie had stood side by side with the girl they would be almost identical save for the hair; Natalie's was dark, raven coloured. Yes he knew they were sisters, but they weren't twins, not in the real sense of the word. But standing here now it had a creepy, almost macabre, effect.

'What do you want?' he finally croaked, wondering if Natalie could hear the conversation or whether she was too absorbed in her private matters upstairs.

'Just wanted to catch up with my sister you know, introduce myself.'

'Get out.' The man said through gritted teeth, managing to keep his voice low, not wanting to alarm his daughter. He was shaking, both inside and out, and all he wanted to do was run; there was something emanating from this woman that was not evident in the pictures he had acquired of her.

In the pictures it was the eyes pure and simple.

They were dark and empty and had that same appearance as

Bundy and West. Whether it was hate or utter unfathomable evil that lurked there he wasn't sure. But with this woman standing in front of him he understood wholly, she was rotten to the core, evil through and through. Whatever had begun in her father had found its way to his first born daughter.

He took a step back.

She took a step forward, a grin of menace etched over her features, her eyes thirsty for harm.

'Leave us alone.' His voice was rising in both tone and volume.

'Too late for that George.' she said, her voice feigning that of a lost innocent wanting nothing more than to find her way home. 'I just want to meet my sister, be a family like you are, is there anything so wrong in wanting that?'

'Leave us alone,' he repeated, his voice rising a notch.

Maggie Dean simply grinned.

In one action she moved forward as if to make a grab for him.

George Soderman spun on his heels and made to run but caught his heel on the base of the hallway table. He fell to the floor with a crash and immediately Maggie Dean was upon him, sitting in a crouch above his chest. She leant into his face, so close that he could taste her fetid breath that was an indication of her inner self; bad and rotten.

'Better get used to the idea of being on your own George.'

From upstairs came the sound of a door opening and a voice disturbed Maggie's enjoyment.

'Dad, you okay?' Natalie called from the top of the stairs.

Maggie leant forward and planted a kiss on George's cheek before pushing herself away from him. In the next instant she was gone, heading towards the rear of the house and the door that led into the garden. A fleeting thought crossed George's mind, a notion that this woman knew her way around his house a little too well, that maybe she had been here before. The notion was, like Maggie Dean, gone in an instant.

George pushed himself up on to his elbows and tried to respond to his daughter but he was breathless, shaking all over and his mind was hazy and unclear.

'Dad?' Natalie called again, this time more urgently. He vaguely heard the sound of her ending the call and rushing down the stairs. Climbing to his feet he used the wall for support and was edging into the kitchen to the chair when the pain in his chest exploded like a rocket and he fell to the floor with a thud.

The last thing George Soderman recalled was his daughter's ashen face gazing down at him in utter despair. Then everything went black.

Chapter 18

Paul Williams was used to calls in the middle of the night; he was equally used to the look of annoyance that emanated from his wife as he kissed her goodbye, explaining that the disturbance was once again down to the alarms at the office as she rolled over and went back to sleep with a groan of irritation.

Having dressed quickly and doing his best not to wake the kids, Williams had driven the short distance from home to office. He had spoken to the alarm receiving centre en-route who had stated that the call was marked down as unknown intruder at which point a notion went off in Williams' brain and he suddenly knew the identity of the nameless prowler.

Shaking his head with frustration Williams had ended the call and thought of the decorators who had been in the office earlier that evening. He had attended a similar call last week when they had first started the paint job; he had hoped that it would have been the last warning given, especially with the words he had exchanged with the head contractor.

Pulling up outside the office, Williams took a deep breath, looked at the clock display and grumbled his displeasure at having to be at work at such an unholy and early hour; it was not that long after 6am.

Hell, it was still bloody dark, he mused as he got out of the car, taking his torch with him making another mental note to get some outside lights installed. He gave the exterior of the building a quick once over, running the beam of light over the scaffolding and boards that had been erected to allow the painters access to the entire rear of the building. If truth be told Williams had not been happy about the scaffolding, thought that it would be like a moth to a flame as the saying went, an irrepressible lure for both adolescents and potential burglars alike, but he didn't have much option. The work had to be done.

Williams felt his mouth turn into a smile, but it was a smile that held no joy, for the shaft of light located the rear window that was slightly open. It was a window from the corner of Harry's office, a window where the decorators had been working yesterday evening.

Shaking his head, frustration combined with irritation, he made a mental note to contact the building contractor on Monday, he was damned if he was going to start worrying about sending an email now, especially as it was the weekend.

Quickly he unlocked the door and bustled his way through.

He was all poised to shut off the alarm but no piercing sound met his appearance. Odd, he thought, turning on the hallway lights and checking the alarm panel. The display was littered with error messages, mostly relating to the ground floor, the offices of Harry Stone.

It was as he turned to look at the doorway that led into the investigators office that he noticed the door was ajar. Harry never left the door anything but closed. He was to some extent fanatical about security, always saying that the files on his clients had to be secure at all times. Williams knew that one of the first things Harry had implemented upon inheriting the firm was to have the place as paperless as possible. Out went the reams of paper and the cabinets full of folders holding client information. In its place appeared the highly priced and highly secure document and scanning management system. The result was a tidier and more spacious office. In fact, the office was probably too large for them now. The final work had been completed prior to the Christmas break and over a festive drink Harry had told Williams about the final piece of his office jigsaw, the addition of a system whereby his client data, the lifeblood of his firm, was now replicated to another server in another city in the

UK. It meant that if disaster struck and the office was raised to the ground, Harry and his assistant could simply set up in a temporary office, his own home if required, and they would have instant access to their client information. As Harry had put it that evening, this was disaster recovery in its most ingenious and reliable form.

As Williams reached the doorway he paused.

What if someone was inside?

What if they were waiting ready to strike?

Backtracking ever so slightly, Williams pulled his mobile phone from his pocket and dialled Harry Stone's number.

* * *

The roads were deserted as Harry made his way from home to the office. It was Saturday morning, just before 7am, and a time when most normal people were in bed asleep. Not that that same rule applied to the investigator, he had awoken in his chair just short of 3:30am. He was cold and a dull ache issued from his neck where he had slept at an odd angle.

When his mobile phone had begun ringing three hours after he had woken up, he looked at the device quizzically, as though he had never heard his phone ring. His haze of confusion had lifted the instant he saw that it was Paul Williams ringing. As well as being a friend and a cohabiter of the building in which he worked, Williams was also the key holder for the alarms. And if Williams was ringing this early on a Saturday morning there was only one explanation for it.

After a brief phone conversation and an even quicker bathroom stop, Harry had grabbed his keys and headed for his office.

There was nothing unusual about him going to the office of a weekend; he spent most Saturday and Sunday mornings going over the cases and trying to make plans for the coming week. This morning proved to be different though.

When he arrived, Harry found the police and Williams waiting on the doorstep.

Lights were on in his office so he guessed the police had searched them and the lack of any worried expressions etched over their faces told him that no one had been found lurking.

'Sorry for the early morning call Harry.' Williams began, and before he could continue Harry held up his hands in mock surrender.

'No need to apologise, thanks for the call. I take it you found no one inside?' The police constable and Williams nodded their agreement without uttering a word. 'Is there any damage?' Again the pair of men followed their synchronised nodding. 'At least that's something.' Whilst Williams spoke with the policemen regarding the crime incident number, Harry entered the building and the entranceway to his office. He stood in the doorway wondering what in the hell's name the intruder, or intruders, were looking for. Was it perhaps kids on a late night prank or was it something more sinister connected to one of his cases? Paranoia always crept in when something out of the ordinary happened.

Hearing the sound of footsteps behind him Harry turned to see Paul Williams standing in the doorway to the offices of Hunter Stone & Co. His face was a mixture of awkwardness and unspoken regret. Harry cut him off before he had a chance to speak.

'It's okay Paul, nothing missing and no damage done.'

'That's not the point, bloody decorators; I will speak to the guy in charge again on Monday, especially given what has happened.'

'How long before they are finished?' Harry asked standing in the opening to his office, looking at the open doorway and lit room that was their meeting room.

'A few days hopefully. Sorry once again Harry.'

'It's okay, probably just kids mucking around.'

Just inside of the entrance to the investigator's office was the photocopier and beyond that his own office. The office was smaller than when his predecessor had been in residence, mainly due to the fact that the far end of the office had been separated off with a small air conditioned room which housed his computer system and various internet links that connected him to the outside world.

As he moved into his office, and in the silence of that moment, he heard the low hum of computer equipment; he discarded his coat and dropped it down on his desk then turned and faced the facilities manager.

'Fancy a brew whilst we're both here?' Williams relaxed and returned the smile, nodding his agreement at the idea. Harry left his office and ushered Williams past the two reception chairs and table, he paused at the sliding door which separated the main portion of the office from the meeting room and his own office.

The kitchen area was small but met their needs; it consisted of a sink, draining board and enough space for a quick boil kettle and toaster. There was a double cupboard above which housed the client cups and a few other essentials, and a single cupboard below which was empty save for the cleaning products his assistant liked to keep on hand. Harry smiled, amid all the insanity of his days, Val Hardy was his saviour. She kept the office running, took some of his meetings and, he felt quite sure about this, could have made a hell of a career as an investigator herself if the desire would have taken her. Fortunately for both Harry and the former owner of the business she had decided against it and instead kept them in check.

'Coffee?' Harry asked, boiling the kettle and taking two mugs from the cupboard. From his office he heard the sound of his mobile ringing. 'Popular today,' he muttered, adding coffee to both mugs and deciding to leave the caller in the safe hands of his voice mail this time.

Chapter 19

Natalie ended the call the moment the computerised voice had cut in. God how she hated voice mail messages, instantly criticizing herself considering the fact that she herself used the automated message system all the time both to leave and to take messages. A half smile creased her pale and tired features as she admitted, and not for the first time, that she was after all the product of an overly technological age, never offline, persistently online, always available. A curse of the modern age she thought.

Standing outside the hospital, the sky was grey with the light patter of rain enveloping the handful of staff, patients and visitors who were either smoking, waiting for their lift or just getting some fresh air.

In Natalie's case it was fresh air and thinking time.

Everything had happened like the whirl of an emotional tornado. It was almost a blur, an agonizing and worrying sequence of events that had begun the moment she had set foot back in the house after her walk into town.

Her father was troubled, that much was evident.

The fact that he wanted to sit down with her and tell her something important was more proof if ever she had needed any. As he had begun to speak her phone had rung, it was one of the investigators with news about the break-in at her flat; she had recognised the number instantly. At that point she knew that she had to take the call. She had apologised to her father by way of silent words before she had left the room, feeling bad that she had interrupted her father's heart to heart but knowing that she had to get an update on her life in London. As she left the room she wasn't sure if the look on his face was disappointment or relief, she guessed maybe a little of both.

She had been upstairs on the call when she thought she heard her father calling out to her. He had not shouted her name again so wondered if perhaps all she had heard was a trick of the mind. But as she was listening to the police officer at the end of her phone, telling her not to worry, that they were doing everything they could, Natalie felt sure that she had heard movement downstairs. With hurried pleasantries to end the call and hearing promises to keep her updated, she had ended her call and rushed downstairs. That was when she had seen her father walking, no change that, staggering, on unsteady feet, the next moment he had crashed to the floor. Everything after that seemed to happen so fast, as though her body had taken over when the shock of what was happening had set in.

She had ridden in the ambulance with her father, anxious, upset and wishing that her mother was by her side instead of being alone. Her mind had raced ahead at a thousand thoughts a minute, wondering if he would pull through, if he was okay, could she have done anything quicker.

It had been as the ambulance had screeched into the A&E parking area that her father had begun to come around and began muttering almost soundless words, his eyes searching her out. To catch his hushed words she had had to lean forward in order to understand but his words came as delicate whispers, as though his voice had been muted.

Finally, as Natalie heard the voices of the paramedics and the opening of the rear doors his voice reached her ears.

'I need Harry Stone.' He said before lapsing back into silence, the effort of the message demanding too much in his current state. In the next instant he was rushed from the ambulance and in through the accident and emergency doors, Natalie trailing in his wake, wondering what the hell was going on and what Harry Stone could do to help the situation.

* * *

Checking the time display on her mobile she realised that so much had happened in so little time. It was just after 7am, she had been here all night. She had been told to go home and rest, that her father was stable and in safe hands, but something in her told her not to. Something deep rooted told her to stay as close to her father as possible. Perhaps it was what had happened to her mother, perhaps it was her guilt at not being there when her mother had collapsed, that she had missed seeing her mother in those final moments, unable to say a proper goodbye, to offer a final "I love you", a final sentiment of love in death.

Wiping a tear from her eye, Natalie went back inside, pausing only to collect another refill of coffee from the vending machine. The thick, almost syrupy, liquid was hard to swallow and bitter in taste but it was coffee; it would keep her awake, that was for sure.

Her thoughts moved from coffee and returned to Harry Stone. As if the doorway into her past had been pulled wide open by her return home so that long since forgotten memories flooded out, bursting the riverbanks her mind had built up. Now she remembered where she had known him from: senior school. He had been above her by a couple of years, back then he was known as Harrison Stone, a loner who communicated only when necessary and who was often seen out on the running track, running as though there was some place he had to be, a place he never had any chance of reaching as his final destination.

Her father had murmured Stone's name several times after being admitted to hospital but since then he had been quiet. It was in one of those moments that the nurse had heard the name of Harry Stone mentioned and had shown a sign of recognition at the name. When Natalie pressed the nurse, asking to know more of the relevance of the man, she found the nurse was only too happy to offer an answer. The nurse didn't necessarily know Stone, but knew of him. As she spoke she gave off that youthful flush that the young often did when speaking of someone they fantasised about.

'Stone runs a private investigation firm in town; there was an article in the local paper a while back after he reopened his offices. Apparently he inherited the firm when the owner passed away. A good looking guy if you ask me.' The flush hit full colour as the nurse turned away in an effort to try and hide her embarrassment but failed. Natalie smiled briefly.

Natalie had thanked the nurse, the mystery deepening. She had stored the information away and later when she was outside taking a break, she had placed a quick call to directory enquiries and was then put through to the number she had requested. Not that it mattered, Stone still didn't pick up her call and deep down she probably had not expected him to considering it was on a Saturday morning, but then again you never knew with these investigator types, always on call wasn't that their motto? Instead the androgynous voicemail system cut in and she had ended the call, not wanting to leave a message, wanting to speak to the man in person.

Her thoughts had fluctuated between Harry Stone and her father's folder, the same folder that he had been looking at in the study, the very same one that was always hidden when she entered the room. It was also the same folder that still remained on the kitchen table where he had left it after collapsing.

With a quick glance at her watch, Natalie decided that once she had finished her coffee and checked on her father she would head home for a shower and a change of clothes, whilst there she would also grab the folder, it was time to see what her father was hiding inside. She wanted to know what mysteries were contained within and why it was always hidden from her.

Between seeing the contents of the folder and speaking with Harry Stone she felt sure her questions would find the answers she craved.

It was time to do a little bit of investigating of her own.

Chapter 20

Mary Addison and her husband John had been running the Bridge Road Hotel for the last three years. Away from the centre of the main village, the Jacobean inspired hotel with its decorated gables and curved turret to the left of the property, sat at the end of a short gravel track with an ornate water fountain erected in the centre. The front of the building, with its criss-crossed leaded windows that looked out over the driveway, hiding the dining room on one side and a lounge on the other, gave the place both a sinister yet welcoming look. It was just after 8am and Mary Addison stood in the kitchen waiting for the chef to arrive; he was late, again. It was quiet this time of year, always was, and of the eleven bedrooms they had available for use, only three were currently occupied. They had an elderly couple on a weeklong break, a young couple who looked barely old enough to be out on their own – but their ID had said different, and a young single woman who gave the owner the heebie-jeebies whenever their eyes met.

She had been here before; in fact this was the third time she had been. She signed herself in as Margaret Jackson and was, according to the briefest of exchanged conversation, looking to buy a property in the area. Mary had guessed as much; she had seen the girl looking at the local property pages maps and such-like. Mary had also heard that she had been to one of the estate agents in town to gather details. That also accounted for why Mary had seen the young woman sitting in a parked car just off of Hayward Way, although to her own mind she couldn't recall any properties that were up for sale along the road.

Her mind quickly wandered, as it so often did, to George Soderman. Word had spread like wild fire, and it wasn't long before news of Soderman's collapse had reached as far as the hotel.

Her mind wandered again as she heard the sound of footsteps in the hallway that led from the rear set of rooms, past the doorway to the kitchen and then on to the dining room.

It was only fleeting but Mary saw enough of the shape to know that it had been Margaret Jackson walking past the door. She cursed under her breath and looked again at the clock. At that moment John entered the kitchen with a knowing smile etched over his face.

He planted a kiss on his wife's forehead and without exchanging any further words took the chef's apron from the hook behind the door and tied it around him, ready for action,

'Looks like it's me and thee this morning then,' he said finally, firing up the gas burners on the oven and taking a pack of bacon and eggs from the fridge.

'I'll just go and put my hair up.' With that Mary left the kitchen to retrieve a hair band from behind the reception desk. It was as she stood at the desk where guests signed in and out, that she saw the young woman.

She was standing at the doors that led out onto the side veranda.

Mary couldn't put her finger on it, but something was not right with the young woman on this visit. Maybe it was her eyes, those dark pools of the unknown, one minute the look of friendliness, the next moment a flicker of something else that lay behind them, anger maybe, or was it sadness?

She hardly ate nor drank; she spent most of the time out of the hotel only to return with the onset of dusk. Of an evening she would sit in the lounge with a glass of wine that would inevitably be left half drunk, she would flip through random magazines, always with a look of having something else more pressing on her mind.

Mary couldn't put her finger exactly upon what made her uneasy, but the goose bumps that prickled her skin told her enough; it was an intuition that had served her well throughout her life. As Mary located her hair band and tied it in a ponytail, the young woman turned around and met her stare.

The goose bumps came again, as did the ice cold rush of unease through her veins.

The Bridge Road Hotel's sole single female guest said good morning as she walked towards the dining room, and at that moment Mary Addison recalled a vivid memory of a girl from a long time ago, a girl who had bullied her way through school and into adult life.

The same girl who had made Mary's life a living hell for years, the same girl who stubbed cigarette butts on her arm and bruised and blemished her skin with stabs of a compass or the thwack of a wooden ruler. It was also the same girl who could smile sweetly and project the epitome of innocence. The same girl who had died before reaching her eighteenth birthday, the victim of a system that failed her.

Mary Addison returned to the kitchen, ignoring the woman who sat alone, and busied herself with preparing the breakfast. The girl was only booked in for one more night; one more night and she would be gone, normality resumed.

Chapter 21

Maggie Dean sat at the table not feeling very hungry but knowing she had to eat. She was angry and frustrated, both by the fact that Drake had not contacted her with news, coupled with the lack of a paper trail which she had hoped to find in Stone's office.

When she had visited his office in the early hours wondering about breaking in, she had thanked her lucky stars when she had seen the window at the back not properly closed. The building looked as though it was lacking in proper security, save for the alarm, a sticker on the front door told her that the place was alarmed 24/7; she wondered if that was true or just a ruse to avoid unwanted and prying eyes.

She had entered the building waiting for the alarm to ring out but it hadn't.

She felt a wave of relief; the idea that she would have as much time as she wanted to search the offices, but her initial joy was scuppered early on. She found hardly any paper at all. The papers were either locked away or on a computer system.

As she was deciding whether or not to force the cabinet locks she had heard voices outside.

Fear of being discovered made her flee in the same manner as she had gained access, albeit by the skin of her teeth. She had managed to hide in the dark recesses of the car park whilst the guy with the torch swept his light around. Once he had gone inside she made her exit, unseen by anyone.

Playing with the napkin Maggie cursed her disturbed night. To say she hadn't slept well was a massive understatement. When sleep had finally descended it had been for the briefest of moments, and her dreams were a haze, a muddled and confused yet somewhat complicated mess.

There were flashes of her childhood, her parents, their cramped council estate home, the cold bedrooms and shitty food, the smell of damp and mould. Washing hung from every available doorway and over the backs of chairs. The air was thick with the damp newly washed scent of the cheap detergent her mother used, the kitchen worktop littered with the empty bottles of beer and wine that was the alcoholic haze her parents lived in. There followed the endless recollections of the beatings at the hands of her father. The odd slap here and there, no apology, just a look of enjoyment, as though dishing out his own brand of discipline was a source of entertainment for him.

Memories of being shut in her bedroom when the electricity had been turned off or when debt collectors were banging on the front door, her parents conveniently out, no doubt in the local pub, leaving their daughter to hide from fear of being found. Several times the debt collectors, all large bodied men with the air of brutality about them, had left their own brand of calling cards; smashed front door, empty petrol can and box of matches to signify intent.

Were there any happy times? Maggie could not recall them, and as each memory merged into each disenchanted nightmare, she saw the day her world had come falling down around her ears. She saw the police downstairs talking to the neighbours, saw them look up at the windows of their flat. And finally, the police arriving at their door, the assembled crowd of nosy neighbours looked on to see her father led to the police car. Her mother followed, ranting, screaming, denouncing the lies and the wickedness that people spoke of but if she was truthful her mother knew exactly what her husband had been up to, she always had.

And as the night merged into the breaking of a new day, Maggie thought of the endless sessions of therapy, of constant questions, of constant scrutinising as though she were some parasite in a laboratory being studied by many.

And before her eyes had opened with a silent scream caught waiting in her throat, and before she could throw back the covers that enveloped her clammy and damp skin, and before sleep was stolen, Maggie saw the image of her sister, the sister with the perfect life. The sister who had everything she had so badly wanted.

Natalie!

Her mother had been carrying her sister at the time of the arrest, unbeknownst to her, and as the walls had come crumbling down around the family, so grew the second seed of a brutal man.

She never knew her sister, didn't want to get to know her.

For Maggie, Natalie represented a life she could have had instead of what she had been dealt. For Maggie, Natalie represented a life stolen.

Feeling her temper threatening to rise, Maggie dug into her pocket and pulled out her mobile phone. There was a message waiting for her. She hadn't heard the phone beep, must have been whilst she was in the shower. Quickly she scrolled through her messages and opened the flashing envelope.

It was from Drake.

She read the message.

Chapter 22

Robbie Drake had pulled into the service station with the intention of getting some fresh air, some food and maybe hanging back for a bit, in no rush to head back for his meeting with Maggie.

But his nerves had put pay to that.

He had done the job, hell he had had to do the job.

His hand had been forced somewhat. At the exact moment he had decided to creep from the flat she had woken up. She looked a mess; her eyes were filled with the alcoholic haze of a has-been, a wino from the streets. Whether it was seeing him going to leave, or perhaps she read the look on his face, either way it lit the fire that stoked the explosion.

The fury and the words that had erupted from her mouth shocked him, but at the same time he could see the resemblance between mother and daughter so clearly it was frightening.

Without thinking, the whole thing now a blur, he had reached out to halt the attack she had launched on him, but it was no good. His temper had frayed, his patience had been lost. Finally his fist had curled and had shot out, the result was instant. She had fallen back and collapsed to the floor. Pulling his gloves from his pocket he had quickly pulled them on before tightening his hands easily around her throat. Adrenalin fed and quietened his fear.

Beneath him she squirmed, but her strength was nothing compared to his.

Almost as soon as it had started it had ended.

The fight was lost.

Angela Glover lay motionless on the floor of her flat.

In the days to follow, neighbours would admit both publicly and privately that her demise and how she had come to end her days was of no shock, the only astonishment was that it had not happened sooner.

Just the thought of what had happened had made his heart begin to beat faster than normal, too fast some would say. He felt sick and the threat of hot bile rising in his throat was close to spilling. Sweat had been pouring from his forehead and his shirt was virtually stuck, uncomfortably, to his back.

With the car now parked, he opened the window and took in one deep lungful of air after another whilst wiping his forehead with the sleeve of his shirt.

His mobile phone lay discarded on the empty passenger seat, it had beeped a long while ago but he hadn't had the courage to read the message yet. As he looked at the time display on the dashboard he saw that it was mid morning and the Saturday traffic was not as bad as he had first thought. At this rate he would be home within the hour, and the first thing he was going to do was to stop by the 24/7 shop close by and pick up a crate of beer.

Only then could he contemplate meeting with Maggie as she had suggested.

He knew he was a fool, blinded by lust not love and from the first time he had seen Maggie he knew that he wanted her in a way he had never felt for anyone before. It was his weakness, something he was not used to admitting he had.

Maybe it was what they had in common; having come from care homes and being pushed from pillar to post, unwanted, passed on. He knew her anger that was fixated on her sister and the life her sister had. He had brothers, three to be precise, and the three of them lived up North, their life full and rich in terms of family and money and professional lives.

He had not been so lucky. He had been the proverbial black sheep of the family.

An arrest early on for burglary coupled with various other minor offences and his path appeared to have been set. When he had met Maggie Dean some eight years ago he had felt her pain and fallen head over heels for her. He always thought his fondness for her was borderline obsessive, but she didn't seem to mind and he enjoyed what they had. Drake had never been one for music or film but when Maggie mentioned some music she liked or a film she had seen he would follow suit. He would lay his hands on the music and the film by any means possible, just to create closeness with her, a shared interest, a bond of sorts.

It was a dangerous feeling. A dangerous obsession.

He had done, and would continue to do, anything she asked of him, as long as she kept her promise. The promise she had made when he had offered to help her locate her family and take vengeance on them. They were due to meet this evening, and she had asked him to clean up, suggested a hair cut and a shave. His mind was running on overdrive.

Later this evening Drake would have what he had always wanted.

Maggie Dean.

Chapter 23

He had been working his way through his emails for some forty minutes when he heard the sound of car horns and voices outside his window. Leaning forward to part a section of the blind, Harry Stone looked out to see a mini-bus full of OAP's being led from the bus and off in the general direction of the local theatre that was along from the law firm building that was his view.

He was about to let the curtain fall into place when he saw her.

The young woman was standing at the corner of the walkway that led around both front and back of the law firm Paul Williams worked for. She looked undecided, as though she was caught in two minds about something. Her dark hair was pulled back in a ponytail and her ankle-length winter coat was open to reveal a black sweater and black jeans.

He sat there staring for what seemed to be an age.

As the woman looked over in the general direction of his gaze he let the curtains fall back into place, the sudden realisation that he was acting like some peeping Tom rushing through his mind.

Natalie Soderman was more beautiful than any of the pictures her father had shown to Harry. Her pale features were both fragile and misleading; they held an intensity of resolve that he found both alluring and beguiling yet troubling. Troubling because this was a case he was working and one of his rules had been never to mix business with pleasure, at any level, or let his mind be led anyplace other than the case in hand.

George Soderman had told Harry that she had attended the same school as he had but was in a different year to him. He didn't recall the name or the girl from his schooldays, but then again he was hardly a social animal, he had been more akin to the singular life. A few friends but none labelled as his best or closest or however people branded them.

In the back of his mind he heard a voice speaking with a tone of misadventure and mischievousness; *But she isn't your client, her father is!*

He realised that he had stopped breathing and let out a gasp of air at the same moment he heard her footsteps outside his office. Harry wondered if her father knew that she was here. He guessed probably not.

George Soderman had wanted to keep as much as possible from his daughter by way of her blood relatives' past. Or at least until the mess had been put right, when it was safe to tell, to reveal all and lay it to rest once and for all. But why was she here? Had George finally told her everything, or perhaps just some? Surely he would have warned Harry if that was the case? Digging into his pocket he pulled out his mobile and scrolled through the list of numbers until he found the one he wanted, he pressed dial and waited for George to answer.

* * *

Natalie Soderman felt the mobile vibrate in her coat pocket and quickly recovered the device. Her father's phone was a relic by modern day standards, but it still did its job, and the current one was to show that H Stone Mob was calling.

She let it go to voicemail and waited a further few seconds before dialling the command to retrieve the message from the message store to see if one had been left or perhaps the investigator had the same phobia of messaging systems as she did.

There was one message waiting.

Natalie had no idea what she was going to say to the investigator, about what she had read in the folder or about her father being taken ill. All she knew was that Harry Stone was the only other person who could help her, and if her father trusted Harry implicitly, and it appeared that he did, then she would too. She had to. Besides, her father still wanted to see Stone, that request had not abated; if anything, it had merely intensified.

Having returned home from hospital after spending the night at her father's side, Natalie had showered and changed, eaten toast and drunk coffee (more out of need than hunger) as she had spread the contents of the folder out over the kitchen table.

It was a lot to take in, but at the same time it simply made sense.

Her foster parents had never hidden the fact that she was fostered, quite the opposite, and they had been honest in saying that her biological father had served time in prison. But that was all she needed to know, she had never craved any more history or any further element of her past. She was simply happy to be where she was, and happy to be with George and Mary, her parents. She had been given up for adoption for a reason and for Natalie she had no desire to take a trip into the past. She had never wanted to.

She had been told that she had a sister but she had no great hunger to search her out either.

What she hadn't known about was that both George and Mary knew the whereabouts of her sister and of her parents.

Natalie played the message and listened.

* * *

Harry was pacing his office wondering why George had not returned his call. In fact he could never actually recall his voicemail cutting in before. Something didn't sit right with the investigator. Leaning across his desk he peered out of the window, George's daughter was no longer there. He breathed a sigh of relief. It was a complication he didn't need.

He let the blind fall back into place and quickly locked his computer screen and turned off the monitor. Grabbing his coat and keys, Harry Stone locked the office and headed for the door.

As he pulled open the main door to the building he pressed the redial button on his mobile and tried to contact George Soderman once more. As he shut the door he saw the reflection of her red coat in the window.

'Harry Stone?' she said.

He turned and gazed into those dark eyes and pale features. Clutched to her coat was a beige folder with what he could see was George Soderman's careful and neat handwriting over the front.

The phone in Natalie's pocket began vibrating again.

She pulled the phone from her pocket and held it out to the private investigator.

'I think we need to talk.' she said, ending the call.

Chapter 24

Harry Stone looked on impassively as Natalie lowered her eyes and concluded telling the investigator how much she knew. Harry's conscience briefly flirted with a thought of what George would say if he knew that he was sitting with his daughter going through the contents of the folder he had desperately strived to keep from her and from him at first.

Before George's daughter had begun, Harry had made coffee and shown her through to the meeting room. There they had spread out before them the contents of the folder she had handed across to the investigator with what he thought of as reluctance, but maybe it was the reticence of learning something further that she really didn't want to know.

Strewn across the oak veneer table top they stared at the collection of newspaper articles, reports (his own and George Soderman's) as well as pictures of the Glover family prior to the father's incarceration, rough sketches of a family tree with dates and details written in George's small neat hand. Harry followed the line of Natalie's gaze; she seemed to have focused on an ancient press clipping that was brown with age. He meant to lean forward and move the article out of sight but he was too slow, Natalie beat him to it, snatching it out of reach of the man sitting next to her, she began reading.

She lowered the piece of paper and her mouth gave a lopsided grin, it was a look that Harry couldn't read. Instead he averted his eyes for a moment and took a sip of now tepid coffee.

'Now I understand why,' she said, handing the article back to the investigator, her voice low almost a whisper.

'What do you...?' Natalie cut him short with a look that said "don't lie and bullshit me, I know". It was that look in her eyes he had noticed when she was outside, that hardened resolve.

'I understand why dad was trying to hide this stuff, why he didn't want me to read the articles.'

'I'm sorry...' Harry said, meeting her eyes for only the briefest of moments. She took the article back from Harry and ran her eyes over the text. He guessed that she was not reading so much as looking at the faded grainy picture of her blood father that was printed above the main body of the article. He couldn't begin to understand what was going through her mind, what her emotions were, but he wanted to help in any way he could, in whatever way he could. For some strange and inexplicably alien reason, he wanted, needed, to offer support to her. Harry found himself drawn to her and that sensation alone worried as well as thrilled him.

'Talk about dysfunctional.' She laughed but without a trace of humour in her tone. 'You always wonder what happened to your parents when you find out that you've been adopted but something inside of me always told me that I didn't need to know, that I was better off not knowing, but this...' she let the sentence trail off to silence.

Harry remained quiet; he had the awful premonition that she was going to lose it. That the information she had just read about her blood father was all too much, that coupled with her foster father being in hospital and her sister's unrelenting vendetta against her, all for reasons she herself did not understand.

'I'm sorry,' he said again, unsure why he had uttered those useless words but feeling the need, the necessity, to fill the void between them with some kind of sound.

Natalie looked at the investigator who she had known of almost twenty years ago in school. The young boy from back then had changed little in adulthood, save for the obvious. His features were handsome and kind yet his eyes still held something of the unknown; one minute they could be smiling eyes filled with trust and friendliness the next they looked cold, perhaps lost, as though a thousand and one worries were frantically dancing behind them. He still wore his hair to the collar of his shirt, a mousy brown colour that was showing flecks of grey. She felt sure that it had been the same style he had had in school.

The silence stretched until Harry stood up from the table and paced the room.

He took her coffee cup and asked if she wanted a refill.

'Thank you,' she uttered in a voice she barely recognised as her own. But she wasn't sure if she was thanking him for the coffee or perhaps for his presence, for him being there to help her, for being honest with her despite the forced hand.

Natalie followed the man out of the meeting room and out through the reception seating area to the kitchen. Whilst Harry busied himself with making fresh coffee Natalie looked absently around the large open expanse of office. She marvelled at the tidiness of the place. The walls looked as though they had only recently been painted and, save for the windows at the rear, which looked as though they had seen better days, the place could pass for hospital clean.

She walked over to a large wall with a sign indicating that the toilet facilities were found to the left, whilst a double filing cabinet lay closed and, she presumed, locked, protecting all those client secrets. Several pictures in A4 frames adorned the walls and, as she took a closer look, most of them appeared to show an older man with a shock of white close cropped hair and an almost military manner about him.

In half the pictures lurked the presence of Harry Stone, still shying away from people, ever the loner to this day. Natalie, despite the situation she found herself in, realised that she was smiling with warmth and affection for the man who at this moment was making coffee and trying to help her, a man she hardly knew. A man who, as a boy, was something of an enigma. He was courteous and would offer a warm smile if you spoke, yet there was something both fascinating and worrying in those eyes and his general demeanour. It gave him the appearance that something was going on in that mind of his, something that the outsider was not privy to understand. It was the same now as he made the coffee. It was as though the simple act of making a drink gave him time to contemplate, to think. She hoped so anyway; she needed all the help she could get.

* * *

Harry took longer over the coffee than he should have but he needed a few moments to catch his breath, reorganise his mind and to put his thoughts in order. For the past hour Natalie had taken him through her background, what she knew about her blood parents and her current life in London. She left out intimate revelations and was quick to move on when pressed about boyfriends, past and present. Harry wondered if maybe there had been a recent break-up to account for the swiftness in moving the conversation along.

She told him about how her father had been calling his name to which Harry smiled, making a mental note to go see George Soderman as soon as he could.

In turn, Harry had given her the information he had to hand, when her father had employed him and where he was currently at with the investigation. With George in hospital he saw no reason to conceal his information any more. It was a decision he was willing to take.

As he poured the coffee he glanced around and stole a glimpse at the woman who stood looking over the pictures on the wall. She had removed her long red coat as they had entered the meeting room but it was only now that Harry could fully appreciate her slender frame.

He knew from the information that George had given him that she was not married and there was no current boyfriend on the scene. Despite that information he still let his eyes wander over the ring finger of her left hand – she was not wearing one – nor was there any sign of a ring having recently been removed – none.

Natalie turned from the pictures and followed him back through to the meeting room. She thanked him for the drink and resumed her seat, silence descending for a few moments whilst Harry shuffled papers in order to regain his focus, to get his head back to the job in hand.

Natalie's phone rang to disturb the silence.

She answered the call, turning in her seat in order to speak. When the call was finished she turned to Harry with wide and worried eyes.

'It's my father.' She said stuttering her words.

Moments later they were out of the office; papers collected and stored away, coffee left untouched to go cold as Harry Stone drove Natalie Soderman to the hospital as close to the speed limit as possible and as traffic would allow.

* * *

The late Saturday morning traffic slowed their progress at reaching the hospital quickly but Harry did his best to manoeuvre through a mixture of back street shortcuts and dual carriageways. Arriving at the hospital he parked in the first available space, ignoring the signs for "staff only" and promises of clampers close by. They rushed through the entrance past a closed reception desk on one side and a heaving cafeteria on the right. They sidestepped orderlies, patients and visitors alike and took the stairs two at a time. Natalie in the lead, Harry doing his best to keep up. It was as Harry tried to keep up with Natalie's fast pace that he recalled how much he disliked hospitals, their smell, their decor and, he guessed mostly, their threat that this was the last place you would see before departing to whatever lay beyond.

Panting ever so slightly he promised himself that he had to start running again, especially seeing as Natalie obviously kept in good shape, made evident by her speed and lightness on her feet as they made their way to her father's bedside.

When they reached the bed they found it empty and stripped of its covers.

Chapter 25

Movement from the opposite side of her hotel room door disturbed her thoughts. She wondered if it was the maid, seeing as the occupants – an elderly couple who appeared to enjoy the benefits of walking – had gone out in full walking gear shortly after breakfast and looked set for a day of serious hiking.

The room was in semi darkness despite the hour of the day. The curtains were pulled most of the way across the window with only a slender slit of light showing. The television was on but the volume was on low, the flickering of the screen offered the most light and showed the silhouetted figure of the single female occupant who was sitting on the floor with her legs crossed beneath her as her body rocked gently back and forth.

Dressed in a white sleeveless tee shirt and a pair of dark panties she looked absorbed in her own world, lost in thought, or at least she had been until the disturbance from outside of the room.

She felt tired, drained.

Her mind was running a fine line between holding it together and losing it completely.

Why? Because that was how it happens sometimes.

Like when she was being interviewed by the care workers and the therapists. During those times she almost always kept it together, and on the very few occasions that she could feel herself losing it, could feel her blood beginning to boil and the hairs on her body showing signs of prickling with agitation, she bit her lip, hard, and lost herself to another place.

Pushing herself up from the floor she walked across to the door and looked through the peep hole. The door opposite seemed such a distance away when in fact it was merely within touching distance if she opened her door. She saw the maid's trolley and the opposite door open. She heard the sound of laughter, of chatter – the television set had been switched on – followed by the sound of hovering.

Quickly she took the "do not disturb" sign from her room, opened her door and slipped it over the door handle before closing the door without a sound. The maid was the last thing she needed at this precise moment in time.

She returned to the floor, sat down with her legs crossed beneath her and with her hands resting on her knees. She closed her eyes and tried to block the noise from across the hallway out of her mind.

She couldn't.

If anything the noise was getting louder, magnified by a mind that was tired and weary and close to breaking. It was as if the maid was under strict instructions to make as much noise as possible, her sole purpose to disturb the silence.

She bit down on her lower lip, enough to break skin and release a thin trail of blood. The short stab of pain and the coppery aftertaste did little to rouse her from her position, but it was enough to stem the flood of anger that was building rapidly and threatening to spill out in vast proportions.

The hovering stopped for a moment.

The woman looked across at the chair and to the clothes that lay in readiness for later that evening. The jeans were tight and fitted her well; in the past they had drawn the right kind of attention by the wrong kind of eyes, and she was sure that the white top with the thin straps that left little to the imagination would do the same. Everything was set, everything was in place, and the final countdown was beginning.

Her mind felt dizzy with elation.

Could it really be that everything was heading in the direction of her plans made so long ago?

Maggie Dean let a smile spread across her lips as her eyes narrowed.

Across the hallway the maid began her duties once again.

She crunched her knuckles, resolving that perhaps she should take a couple of tablets that would make her sleep; she wasn't meeting Drake until later that evening and she didn't have time for disruptions and complications such as the maid. Deciding against the tablets, Maggie thought that maybe she would take a trip out to Hayward Way and check on the Soderman residence; if no one was in then she could finalise her plans for the coming days.

With a plan formulated within her cluttered mind the frustration abated and a sense of satisfaction returned. Pressing thoughts of Drake and that evening aside, Maggie Dean pushed herself up from the floor and threw on some clothes.

Everything was going to be okay.

Everything was set.

Chapter 26

Natalie spun round looking for a nurse or anyone in a uniform who could help.

'Took your time didn't you?' said the raspy voice that was unmistakably George Soderman.

'Sorry, we got here as soon as we could,' his daughter replied, her voice a mixture of stunned mistrust at seeing her father and an outward show of relief.

'We?' asked the curious voice.

George Soderman was standing over by the window looking out over a paved courtyard decorated with pot plants and chairs. As he turned around to embrace his daughter with a smile he noticed the private investigator standing in the doorway.

'Harry gave me a lift when I got the call from the nurse.' George Soderman looked from his daughter to Harry and back again, it was only when the older man saw the folder in Harry's hand and the look of embarrassment on the younger man's face that he realised the significance of what all this meant.

'Oh!'

'I guess now you can tell me everything instead of trying to handle it all on your own hey?' Natalie said, walking with her father back towards his bed. As Natalie and her father made their way to the bed, a nurse busied herself in the final stages of having remade his bed with fresh covers.

'Harry?' the older man said, looking for confirmation.

'She knows everything now George, sorry.' The old man lowered his eyes to his lap and rubbed his hands together as though contemplating his next words with care and perhaps a little chagrin at his secret finally being known to his daughter.

'I don't understand,' Natalie said, slumping down into a chair next to her father, rubbing her eyes as though the act alone would wipe away the tiredness that her body and mind felt at that moment.

'Darling Nat,' George Soderman said, leaning across to his daughter and placing his hands over hers. 'Would you be able to ask the nurse to bring along a jug of water, my throat is dry as anything.' Natalie smiled and left the room in the same direction as the nurse who had only moments ago left.

'I'm...' Harry started but was quietened instantly by an old man whom he realised had a steely look of resolve in his eyes that had been hidden seconds earlier. The look matched that of Natalie's Harry noted with amusement.

'We have to be quick, Nat will be back shortly.' Harry took his cue and nodded his head in acquiescence, letting the old man speak. 'She was at my house Harry, in my house.' The investigator didn't need to be told who, the look etched over his client's face was enough to tell him all he needed to know.

'I don't know how many times she has been there or how she got in but she is serious about what she will do to Nat, Harry, and I can't have that, I won't have anything happen to my daughter. It would make everything Mary and I have worked for worthless; it simply cannot happen, do you understand?' Harry nodded and thought he detected the slight glint of a tear in the old man's eyes, but before he could get a second look it was blinked away and his eyes lowered back to his lap.

'We have to go to the police now George, this is serious, way beyond finding missing people and way beyond my remit to be honest.'

'No!' Soderman said, his voice barely rising above a whisper but which contained the necessary amount of defiance and power to tell Harry that involving the police was not an option up for consideration or discussion, ever.

In the hallway they heard the sound of voices and footsteps.

'Protect her Harry, please, no matter what, I am begging you. Protect her, that is all I am asking.'

'But what can I...' again his words were cut short, this time by a fleeting look of utter pleading. Despite the portrayal of private investigators in fiction and on film, his career did not involve running into many crime lords, or murderers. Yes he dealt with a few of those persons who lived in the lower echelons of society. Most of his day to day, bread and butter work, was finding missing people. Predominantly it was children, whether they were young or old, and most of the time they had run off after a spat with their parents of one kind or another, or following philandering men and women. With the Soderman case came an entirely different kettle of fish, something he had never covered before and he was unsure of which way to go, of what to do. His first thought at finding out that Natalie was in danger and that Maggie Dean had somehow gotten into the family home, was to speak to the police. To hand over the case and carry on with his current case load that was getting left behind, but he couldn't. He hated giving up on something when he had started it.

He liked George Soderman, maybe because he reminded him of his own father in places; sometimes stubborn, opinionated with concerns of the state and monarchy but deep down a genuine man who meant no harm to man nor beast and gave his all to his family.

Natalie of course was a wholly different prospect. In the pictures Harry had been shown she had looked pretty, of that there was no argument, and of the way her father spoke about her she came across as intelligent and intellectually bright, someone who knew her own mind and didn't take too much crap, from anyone. But then he had met her in the flesh and all that had changed.

'Here you go.' Natalie Soderman said, walking into the room and placing the filled jug of water on his side table.

'Thank you.'

'So?' Natalie said, looking from her father to Harry and back again.

'So what?' her father replied, his eyes not rising to meet hers, looking more like the young boy who had been caught stealing sweets from the sweet shop than the mature father that he was.

'What was so important that you wanted to have Harry rushed here and that is so secret that you have to send me away on wild goose chases for fresh water? I thought there were no longer any secrets between us, what's up?'

Harry tried, but ultimately failed, at stifling a laugh. In such a relatively short space of time he had spent with the woman, he liked her more and more.

* * *

By the time Harry had returned to his car, thankful that there was no parking ticket stuck to his windscreen or a yellow clamp over any of his tyres, he felt drained, both emotionally and physically. He opened the door and climbed in, turned the ignition and switched on the CD player. The CD bay was empty and he suddenly recalled taking the CD that had been in there into the house a few days before.

Leaning forward he opened the glove compartment and took out two cases, both of which he realised Paul Williams had lent him some time ago. He made a mental note to return them next week with sincere apologies.

Deciding on Radiohead he slotted the CD into the player and waited for the opening track to start. He lent his head back against the head rest and closed his eyes for a moment whilst his mind wrestled with the details of the Soderman case.

If his predecessor was here he would know what to do. Laurence Hunter had seen it all during his forty years in the private investigation business. He had had his fair share of missing persons and cheating spouses, but he had also dealt with several high profile cases that had made the national newspapers, one which came to mind instantly on reflection. The case had been in the late 1970s and was initially a missing persons case, the mother – Fiona Thomas – had walked out of the house late one night and not returned. No arguments, no money troubles, nothing on the surface of a normal marriage. The husband – Peter Thomas – had been at work when his wife had gone missing and had been for several hours.

It was only as the case opened and the days drew into weeks that it was found that Fiona Thomas had been planning to leave her husband. Not for another lover, simply because she was bored and loved him no longer. Peter Thomas, not known for his anger of any sort in the local community, had lashed out, knocking the woman from her feet; she had fallen and hit her head on the edge of a table but her husband's brutality had not ended there...

That had been the end of his wife and the beginning of the missing person case.

When finally the body had been discovered, hidden amongst the dilapidated allotment buildings not far from their home, her body was a map of bruises, fractures and decomposition.

Peter Thomas had played a good game of cat and mouse but in the end Hunter had got to the truth and Harry could not but wonder what his late mentor and friend would have done had he been here now.

His thinking was interrupted by a knock on the passenger window. He looked across and saw Natalie standing there. He smiled and motioned for her to open the door. Harry hadn't mentioned waiting for her, hadn't offered to drop her back home, but with her now sitting in his car the words of her father came back to haunt him.

Protect her Harry, please, no matter what, I am begging you.

'Can I drop you home?' he asked, turning down the music and turning the key in the ignition

'If you don't mind, otherwise I can grab a taxi or wait for the bus.'

'No that's fine.' Harry eased the car out of the parking space and headed out of the hospital complex. The afternoon sky was darkening with the promise of rain to come. The unlit road masked the interior of the car in black which left both occupants to their own thoughts.

In the background Thom Yorke's wounded lyrics brought his angst-ridden vocals to life, and Harry wondered if maybe he should change the CD to lighten the mood.

'Didn't have you down as a Radiohead fan?' Natalie said, gazing out into the dark borders that flashed by. Harry laughed.

'What did you have me down as?'

'Not sure really, maybe a throwback to eighties rock, perhaps Guns 'N' Roses, Big Country, something like that.' Harry laughed again. 'So come on spill the beans, aside from the torment of Radiohead, what's your taste?'

'A little bit of everything,' he replied, looking across to meet her gaze for the briefest of moments before returning his eyes to the road. The first splattering of rain touched the windscreen as Harry switched on the wipers. 'Have a look in the glove compartment; there are some other CDs in there.'

'No honestly I am fine with this one, although,' she said mischievously, 'I might just have a little look to see what you're concealing.' With that she leant forward and delved into the dark space beneath the dashboard. She clasped a couple of cases and brought them out. Harry switched on the interior light for her.

'Oh now I can see why they are hidden away and why you are so defensive about giving away your musical tastes,' she said with a laugh. Harry couldn't see which one she was looking at, in truth he had forgotten what CDs were even in there, but he liked the sound of her laugh and he liked the easy going conversation, the ridicule of his musical taste he could cope with.

'Mr Stone,' she said, mockingly, holding up two CD cases, one for the soundtrack to Notting Hill and the other a greatest hits compilation of Wham! He couldn't recall Paul ever lending him those two CDs and he certainly didn't recall his ever buying them himself let alone receiving them as gifts.

The conversation continued, moving from music and merging into films. And as Harry pulled into the driveway of George Soderman's home he felt as though he had known Natalie for longer than he had.

He silenced the engine and followed Natalie from the car. It was not until they had reached the front door that Natalie's body seemed to lose her cheerfulness, instead it went rigid, her smile now replaced by a frown of worry and an ever growing sense of unease.

'What is it?' he said trying to read her features.

'It could be nothing.'

'But?'

'It's just that I am sure I didn't leave any lights on, I'm almost sure that I remember switching off the hall light and then locking the front door.'

Harry followed her gaze and saw what she was looking at, the hallway light was on. In the back of his mind he heard George Soderman's voice again. *Protect her Harry, please, no matter what, I am begging you.* He also recalled the man's comments about Maggie Dean having been in the Soderman house. He reached forward and tried the front door.

The door swung open, unlocked.

'Stay here a moment.' Harry said, entering the house.

Chapter 27

George Soderman felt his age and then some as he lay tired and useless in his bed. Nurses moved busily around him and their presence gave him absolutely no chance of slipping away to the payphone or, better still, being able to discharge himself.

He was worried for Natalie and fearful of Maggie.

Maybe he had misjudged her. In fact on second thoughts, there was no *maybe* about it, he had misjudged her. He thought he could scare her off at best, pay her off at worst. But he had been wrong. With her appearance in his own home and having the chance to see into her dark empty eyes he now knew the truth. She *was* her father's daughter and the proverbial apple had not fallen far from that particular tree.

George trusted Harry, trusted him with his life and the life of his daughter, but he had noticed the look that his daughter had given the investigator and the way she had acted around him. Natalie may have been older now but she still suffered the same idiosyncrasies she had when she was a young girl, namely whenever she was around someone she liked she blushed and talked more.

During their visit earlier in the afternoon she had done both to good effect and he had done all he could to suppress a smile or make a comment.

Soderman looked at the clock on the wall and wondered what she was doing.

He had asked Harry to protect her, but he wondered deep down who was going to protect Harry.

Chapter 28

Natalie stood on the periphery of the entrance to her family home not wanting to enter the house but disliking the darkness that was biting at her heels behind her. Harry had completed a search downstairs and had found nothing wrong. A few moments ago he had climbed the stairs to begin a search of the upstairs and as he disappeared from sight she had never felt so alone in her entire life.

'Harry?' she called, not recognising the sound of her own voice and the whispery frightened tone that echoed around the ground floor. From upstairs she heard a movement, seconds later Harry appeared at the top of the stairs looking startled.

'You okay?' he called, looking down over the ground floor.

'Yeah I'm good, I just...'

'You'd better come and take a look at this.' He said, waiting for Natalie to enter the house and climb the stairs to where he was waiting for her on the landing.

It wasn't very often that Natalie was lost for words, but the moment she stared in to her old bedroom she felt an overriding sense of terror coupled with panic rush through her. For a brief moment she felt a wave of light-headedness threaten to steal the power in her legs to send her collapsing to the floor. Recovering slightly she gazed at the room before her.

The room was ransacked to the point that the floor was hidden by the scattering of clothes and belongings. Books were strewn and clothes were littered, it was like a hurricane had whirled through the room. Of course the truth was a little more startling.

Harry had his mobile phone out of his pocket and was already scrolling through his address book to find the number of a contact he relied on when times like these presented themselves.

He knew that George Soderman didn't want to involve the police, that he could understand, but twice in the last twenty four hours Maggie Dean had entered the home, he didn't want there to be a third and with the lack of evidence pointing to a break in there was only one logical reason; Maggie Dean had a set of keys.

As he waited for the call to be answered he watched Natalie as she stood dumbfounded in the doorway, her eyes gazing around the room in despair and horror as her body leant against the frame of the door for support.

'Jeff?' he said when the call was picked up. 'Harry Stone, I have a job for you.'

* * *

They sat at the kitchen table in silence. Natalie held a glass of wine to her lips and took a long drink. Harry was drinking coffee although he was in desperate need of something similar to what the woman across from him was drinking, or maybe stronger. He thought about his bottle of Jim Beam back at home tucked away in the cupboard.

'All I ever seem to be saying to you at the moment is thanks,' she said, looking over the rim of her glass to meet the man's eyes. He smiled without reply. From the hallway they both heard the sound of tools clattering on the floor, moments later a man stuck his head around the door.

'Job's done H.' He said throwing a set of keys towards the man who sat at the table.

'Thanks Jeff, appreciate you coming out so quickly.'

'I'll send the bill to you yeah?'

'You do that.' With that the locksmith said his goodbyes and left. He had replaced locks on the front and back doors as well as fitting security clips to all the lower ground windows. Natalie had offered to pay but Harry told her it was all part of the service, and besides, her father was his client and he was bankrolling his work. Plus he had told Harry to protect his daughter at all costs and this, he felt sure, was a price he would be more than happy to foot the bill for.

As they heard the sound of the work van reversing out of the driveway Harry stood up and took his now empty mug to the sink.

'Harry?' Natalie said, her eyes not looking up from the bottom of her glass. Harry turned and leant against the worktop looking at the woman who sat across from him at the table. She looked so fragile and he wanted to protect her more than ever, to put a defensive shelter around her. He could see she wanted to say something, and for that he didn't blame her, there were probably a hundred and one questions floating around her brain each vying to be let out.

'Is it going to be okay?' she said finally.

The million dollar question had been asked and truthfully Harry didn't know what to answer. In his mind he knew what he *should* answer but he wasn't wholly sure if it was the correct response, or if he could say the words with enough gusto and bravado to offer solace. He liked the girl, he didn't want to overtly lie to her, but at the same time he knew she was now in her most fragile state and needed him more than ever.

'I'm going to do all I can to make sure everything is okay.' He replied, wanting to cross the room and put a hand on her shoulder, or better still to wrap her in his arms and hug her till he himself believed in what he had just said. Instead, he smiled and made as though to get ready to leave.

'Would you stay for dinner?' she blurted out, nearly stumbling over her words as she got up from the table and walked across to meet Harry at the kitchen doorway that led into the hall.

Harry looked at her for a few moments before replying and he saw the desperate truth of the situation and was not surprised by it. Natalie Soderman did not want to be alone this evening and who could blame her, over the past few days, ever since returning home from holiday, her life had been one constant stream of upheaval, unease and bombshells, not to mention the sinister presence of danger lurking close by. As far as Harry could tell she didn't appear to have a boyfriend or significant other that she could ring and ask for help. With her father not wanting to involve the police there really was no one else but himself.

'As long as it's no bother?' he replied, happy to be able to spend more time with her.

'I'm afraid there is not much in so it will be a made up affair, pasta or something with chicken, is that okay with you?'

'Perfect.'

Natalie busied herself in the kitchen, happy it seemed to have her mind occupied by something other than the threat of Maggie Dean and the worrying state of her father. She switched on the radio and began searching for a station that offered something other than classical music or sport updates, Harry sat back down at the table and watched her. If he was honest he wasn't sure if he was more relieved or scared at having been asked to stay for dinner.

For one he hated going home at night to his house that didn't feel like a home and to the chair in the lounge where he would predictably fall into a short sleep; on the other hand he felt his professionalism slipping as he spent more time with her.

He had to remain focused. Didn't want to let his guard down.

He had promised George Soderman that he would do his best to protect his daughter, and that was something he couldn't do if he thought of Natalie as anything other than his client. *But she isn't your client is she?* said a mischievous voice inside his head, a voice he tried desperately to dismiss as quickly as he could.

Having found a radio station that was playing some guitar rock that he didn't recall; Natalie turned to him and held an empty wine glass in his direction.

'Can I tempt you?' she said.

Harry felt himself redden and wasn't sure he could reply with a steady voice, instead he smiled in reply, feeling his professionalism ebbing even further away.

As Natalie poured a glass of wine both she and Harry were oblivious to the face that was watching with irritated rage at the window.

Seconds later the face was gone.

Enough had been seen in those few stolen moments.

Chapter 29

Maggie Dean stood in front of the mirror, a towel wrapped around her middle, and her skin glistening with water having just taken a long hot shower. She had hoped that the searing water would strip away her anger aimed towards her sister. She had to keep her desire to hurt in check; things were not ready yet; she still had things to arrange and take care of before the final act of her vendetta could be completed.

As she had stepped from the shower cubicle she felt that her anger had abated somewhat but her annoyance at herself; her fury at losing her grip was still lurking in the back, nagging away like a jackhammer on a road.

Maggie had simply meant to take a walk to the Soderman house, see if anyone was in, and perhaps have a peek inside once more in readiness for her next visit. But once inside, realising that she was alone, she had been gripped with an overriding desire to search the house, to look at the pictures that gave her a view into the past of the Soderman family. A past that was not hers but her sister's, a life less troubled than her own. There were plenty of pictures of happy times with the three of them, lots of pictures that charted Natalie's rise from childhood to adulthood via family holidays and culminating in the day she finished university and was shown in her gown and rolled certificate clasped to her chest, her cap thrown into the air with pride and elation.

As Maggie had looked into the depths of each picture the fury began to gain momentum.

By the time she had climbed the stairs and stood in the doorway that was evidently Natalie's room, her mind was gone, the dark mist of hatred had well and truly descended and there was little that could be done to stop it.

In an instant she had rushed through the bedroom like a hurricane; pulling books from shelves and scattering them on the floor, ripping clothes from the wardrobe and from an overnight bag that lay at the end of the bed. From a desk she had taken scissors and cut, ripped and stabbed at any of the clothes her hands could find. Her grunts of anger were swallowed by the house, her mind left swimming in a torrent of extreme abhorrence.

As the eye of the storm had finally dissipated, Maggie Dean had collapsed in a ball of spent force to the floor. She had sobbed like a wounded animal, something she had not done in a long, long time. But with the tears came a renewed ferocity of venom, a more focused path for her anger.

She wasn't sure how long she had sat there, but the sound of a car awoke her from her lamentations. Cat-like she was quick to leave the house before the sound of the door opening and voices.

She had loitered around outside, hidden amongst the shadows.

She had watched with amusement as the investigator did the gallant sweep of the house leaving Natalie to stand on the edge of the doorstep to await his command. She mused how easy it would have been to take a knife to her sister's throat before shrinking back to be swallowed by the darkness of the night sky. In that instant it could have all been over. Job done. She could have disappeared from sight, started her life elsewhere as intended. But that was not her plan. That was not how she wanted things to end. It was her way to the bitter end.

As she had waited and watched, what had angered her so was the arrival, not of the police as she thought it might have been, but of the locksmith. Stone was obviously thinking with his head and nothing else, at least for the moment. With the locks changed her means of access and, more importantly, her final plans for dispensing with her sister had been thrown. Access would not be as easy as using her set of copied keys. Now she would have to think of something else.

From the window she had watched them in the kitchen; their closeness, though not apparent to themselves, was obvious to others.

Another problem to be taken into consideration she mused, the silent observer.

After that she had taken the short run back to the hotel, all the while her mind moving from one scenario to another. Her task had now been made that much harder, but she was, if anything, always resourceful.

Taking a breath, Maggie took the dryer from the side and began drying her hair; those issues would have to wait for the moment, as she had to get ready for her evening's entertainment.

Having dressed in her jeans and white top, she pulled her hair into a ponytail and wrapped her coat around her then left her hotel room and the issues of Natalie Soderman temporarily behind.

For the moment she had Robbie Drake to deal with.

* * *

Robbie Drake was many things but even he couldn't hide the nerves that were causing him to pace the apartment he had borrowed from a friend. The place was located in a part of the city where even the police hardly ever dared to visit, without very good reason at any rate.

The upstairs flat had once belonged to downstairs but at some stage they had separated the single building into two flats. The two bed place was small and in need of repair – windows rattled in their frames and leaked heat like a colander, wallpaper circa nineteen seventy was peeling from the walls as damp continued its invasion, whilst in the kitchen units were hanging on hinges that would soon give and come crashing down. In both bedrooms blackened damp spots decorated part of the ceiling like a waiting army that had finally started to advance.

In the lounge/diner/kitchen Drake had tried to make an effort, he had tidied up as much as he could; several bottles of cheap wine littered the kitchen surface as did a selection of takeaway cartons, ready to be reheated when needed.

He looked down at his watch, it wouldn't be long and Maggie would be here. The thought did not settle his already somersaulting stomach; in fact it did the complete opposite. He walked through to the larger of the two bedrooms and checked once more. The covers were neatly set whilst the small bedside table lamp offered a slight respite from the darkness. Returning to the lounge he regained his pacing. Inside his mind was a screaming mass of nerves, telling him that he was useless, that he ought to get a grip. The way he was acting you would have been forgiven for thinking that this was to be the first time that he was to sleep with a woman. The truth was quite the opposite. But tonight was different. Tonight he was getting something that he had wanted for so long, someone he had wanted, craved and desired for a long time.

He had dreamt about this moment.

Sometimes he had even imagined Maggie was the one he was screwing when he had picked up some tart at the end of a drunken pub crawl or found himself stumbling from a club or two.

The nerves though were what threw him. He had done many things in his life that were the epitome of the very darkness of the soul of humanity. If he had been a religious man he would have been in no doubt that the only place he would be going when he left this life was down, down into the burning flames of hell.

He wasn't religious and therefore gave no thought to the dark deeds he had done during his life. He had spent his entire life on a merry rollercoaster of juvenile detention, care homes and prison, none of which particularly phased him but tonight, tonight he was quite simply shitting bricks and it was an alien sensation; it was also a feeling he didn't like; it meant he wasn't in control.

And why? Because it was Maggie Dean, he told himself.

He checked his breath once more but all he could smell was the aftershave from his hands that he had doused over his face.

The doorbell suddenly rang and sent fresh waves of panic through him.

Taking a deep breath Drake tried to compose himself for the evening that was to come. As the doorbell rang for a second time in quick succession he went to let Maggie Dean into his temporary pad.

Chapter 30

Simply put they were drunk. Both Harry and Natalie had drank their way through two bottles of a good Australian red that had been in George Soderman's cupboard. Natalie had cooked some cheese and broccoli pasta with a twist of chilli to give it a kick. They had eaten at the kitchen table whilst the radio continued to play random music, mainly from the nineties and the dawn of the new millennium.

With dinner over they had stacked the plates in the washing up bowl, and despite Harry offering to wash them up Natalie had said that she would deal with them tomorrow, they then moved to the lounge.

Whilst Harry lit the fire Natalie disappeared upstairs to change, reappearing in a pair of dark jogging bottoms and a white sweatshirt.

In the lounge they sat opposite one another on the two seater sofas with the table in between. They chatted easily, the wine alleviating the shyness of one and the worry of the other.

Natalie spoke of her recent trips to Paris and Barcelona and it was evident by the way she spoke and the look that creased her features that she felt a love for the Parisian destination.

'Have you been to Paris?' she asked, looking at him over the rim of another near empty glass.

'Once, a few years back.'

'On your own or with someone?'

'With someone.'

'Girlfriend, friends, boy's trip?' Harry laughed. The entire evening had been conducted in the same manner. They would change topics and begin to talk then all of a sudden Natalie would, with a mischievous look in her eye, fire a barrage of questions that he sometimes found difficult to field. He would find himself stumbling over words, and any chance to change the subject was defied by his interrogator.

Harry had tried to counter the questions with his own, but any attempt to draw answers from his questions on significant others were sternly met with a rebuttal of which there was no chance of change.

In the short time since dinner they had covered music and films, books and television, holiday destinations and favourite foods, they had spoken of school days and of people they still knew and those who had faded away, lost to the past. They spoke of their naivety when it came to the social media sites and how they had so far avoided the lure of Twitter, Facebook and suchlike. The conversation was all too easy, the company enjoyed by both.

Harry liked the way she blushed and lowered her eyes to her glass when he had hit upon something personal. Her laugh made him smile almost as much as the way she played with her hair when anxious. For the first time in a long while he was relaxed around a woman and had no desire to try and be someone he wasn't, and for the first time in a long while he simply enjoyed the company and the laughter, everything else, all his worries of work and private life, put on hold for the moment.

'Sean Connery or Daniel Craig?' she asked, drawing him from his thoughts.

'Easy, it has to be the original James Bond without a shadow of doubt.'

'Hm.' she mused. 'But Daniel Craig did wear those blue shorts very well.' She said, laughing again and blushing at the same time, that mischievousness returning.

He looked down at his watch and caught a disapproving sigh from Natalie.

'Am I boring you?' she asked playfully, leaning forward to place her now empty glass on the coffee table.

'No, no, sorry…'

'It's okay, I was joking,' she said as her voice and tone turned serious for the moment. 'I appreciate you staying with me, I really do. I just didn't want to be…you know…' The sentence trailed to an unfinished end as the CD chose that moment to reach the conclusion of its track listing. For a moment the room was shrouded in silence, broken only by the crackle of the fire which Harry had helped to light earlier.

'Natalie…' Harry began, putting his glass down and standing up.

'Honestly Harry, I'm just thankful to you for arranging the changing of the locks and your company, not to mention your excellent fire lighting skills.' Natalie laughed and stood up, hoping to lighten the mood once more as she followed Harry as he moved towards the door.

'I was just going to ask if you fancied meeting for a drink tomorrow.' Harry wasn't sure how he had sounded, but inside he felt like a schoolboy asking a girl out for the first time.

'I would like that yes.' She replied with hardly any hesitation.

Without any warning Natalie leant in to Harry and pressed her lips against his. If he was taken aback and unprepared he didn't show any signs and gave in to what he had been fighting against all evening.

The next moment all thoughts of leaving disappeared as Natalie pulled Harry tight against her body, savouring his smell and feeling an insatiable and overwhelming need to have his body pressing against hers. Fuelled by a mixture of alcohol, desire and fear, her inhibitions were lost to the moment as she guided him across the lounge and pushed him down upon the sofa.

Straddling him she pulled at his shirt and popped his buttons then tugged at the belt of his trousers, for the moment all thoughts of her sister's vendetta and her hospitalised father left in the far recesses of her mind.

It had been a while since she had felt like this, since she had craved the rough intimacy that making love with a man gave her, and Harry Stone certainly wasn't unattractive. She wasn't sure if it was a mixture of the danger she was in or the fact that she liked his rugged and shy exterior, either way she knew what she wanted as she lunged in and press her tongue deeper into the warm moistness of his mouth.

* * *

He lay spent and clammy, tired yet alive. Next to him she slept, her naked body touching his. He gazed down at her slender frame, now peaceful and calm, unlike the raw passion and desire that had been the frantic love making of before.

Closing his tired eyes he felt the stress evaporate as sleep took hold.

His final image before oblivion stole him was of Maggie Dean's naked body beneath his own as he thrust in time with her frenzied almost animalistic cries, and in the moment that followed, when they appeared to merge into one, as she dug her fingernails into the cheeks of his rump, urging him deeper inside, everything ceased to exit. Outside, the sound of far off sirens mingled with the thud, thud, thud of music from a house down the street and the argumentative screams of a squabbling couple on the pavement nearby simply ceased to be. It was as though they were the last people on an otherwise deserted planet.

But whilst dogs barked and babies cried, Maggie Dean lay awake and smiling. Robbie Drake had performed his final act for her.

From tomorrow her focus was her sister.

She had extended her stay at the hotel by another two nights. Tomorrow she would rest, reassess and prepare for the next part of her plan.

Come Tuesday morning she would have Natalie Soderman with her, one way or the other, and with that thought came an excited smile. Maggie Dean closed her eyes for the moment, allowing her body and mind to rest.

Chapter 31

Harry woke with a scream caught in his throat. The room was cloaked in semi-darkness with moonlight shining through the thin curtains showing a room full of silhouettes. His head had the beginnings of a hangover and his throat felt dry, a result of the red wine he had drunk with Natalie.

He looked across at her sleeping form next to him, her breathing was calm. For the next few moments he lost himself in the simplicity of watching her body rise and fall with gentle rhythm, recalling how only a few hours ago they had been entwined together until both were hot and exhausted from their love making.

A clock on the side table shone its red digits like a set of watching eyes; the time was 03:30.

Harry sat up in bed, trying his best not to disturb Natalie.

Despite the earliness of the morning when most people were asleep, lost in their own dreams – good or bad – Harry felt alive and alert, it was a curse he had got used to over the years. Moving out of the bed he did his best to locate the remainder of his clothes which were scattered over the floor, the rest were downstairs.

He padded carefully out of the bedroom and down the stairs to the lounge where he retrieved his shirt. Dressed, Harry returned upstairs, pausing in the doorway he looked at the undisturbed form of Natalie and smiled.

He hadn't felt like that for a long while, and no matter what happened next, in this moment he felt happy and all other thoughts were lost to the sensation.

On his way out of the house he stopped in the kitchen to write a short note. He left his mobile number and said he would ring her later to arrange meeting later in the day, then he left, driving home without a thought of passing by the office, a rarity in Harry Stone's life.

* * *

As the car reversed out of the driveway and the gravel crunched beneath the tyres of Harry's car, Natalie turned over in bed, absently searching blindly for someone who wasn't there, the empty sheets testifying to his departure. She opened her eyes, pulled the covers around her and moved over to the bedroom window. His car was gone from the driveway.

She felt a mixture of disappointment and acceptance at his early morning exodus. During the course of last night they had spoken of many things, one of which was Harry's insomnia and how he survived most nights on three to four hours of sleep. She recalled her gasp at the sheer disbelief of having less than eight hours but something in his demeanour and the look of fatigue that was barely concealed in his appearance told her that he was not exaggerating.

The more she had come to know the man behind the outward facade that was the dishevelled investigator, the more she realised how little he had changed from his school days. He was still the loner, still happy to get on without fuss or commotion. Yet there was something in his steely eyes that told her he was determined when it came to his profession.

Natalie recalled vague details of his sister's disappearance all those years back and in a funny way she guessed it was apt that he would become an investigator who specialised in missing persons.

When she had pressed him about his missing sister he became reticent, almost uncommunicative to the point of silence. She didn't push the subject much more, but underneath all that she had enjoyed his conversation, his laugh and, above all, his ability to take her mind off her troubles. She hoped that his promise of meeting for a drink later in the day was not the effects of the drink talking.

Seeing the time on the clock and spying the chaos of the strewn clothes and scattered belongings that was her bedroom, Natalie returned to bed. Her mouth felt dry and her head had the dull beginnings of what she knew would be a hangover. Resting her head down upon the pillow she closed her eyes to the growing lethargy, the faint trace of his aftershave engulfing her nostrils. Within a few moments she was gently breathing as sleep stole wakefulness once more.

* * *

Harry felt the burn in his legs but wasn't sure if it was the running or the hangover that was causing him the most misery. After returning home he had sat in his usual chair and contemplated work. It was a fleeting thought, for he had a sudden and almost violent craving, to go for a run.

Back in his schooldays he had been a keen runner, mostly preferring long distance to the sprint races. He thought the metaphor summed up life pretty well, life was all about the long run, the long distance, and those who went off in a sprint evidently never finished the distance or the race.

In the months and weeks since his mother had died, Harry had begun to run more often. He had purchased a proper pair of running shoes, an iPod holder that wrapped around his arm and a fluorescent jacket so even the most deadly of sight-affected drivers would see him on the road and give him the space he needed without running him down.

He had pulled his jogging bottoms and his red sweatshirt from a box that had only recently been opened, retrieved his fluorescent top, music player and keys and set off. It was not long after 6am.

For the first mile he had taken it easy, a canter you would say. He was listening to a playlist that Paul Williams had put together for him, but the tracks were far too mellow and placid for running, he needed something with a bit more bite and a few more adrenalin fuelled guitars blasting into his ears.

He came to a halt on one of the many woodland tracks that

were located in and around the village where he lived. Harry scrolled through the list of artists and came to rest on one he hadn't listened to for a while.

He selected an album by Fountains of Wayne, one of his many early hour iTunes raids where he had purchased several albums that sounded as though they would be good.

Harry selected track two to start with, knowing that this was the kind of music he needed to run to. He pressed play; instantly *Red Dragon Tattoo* began playing, the sound of guitars and bass booming in his ears. With music playing he began running once more, his thoughts all too consumed with Natalie and the night they had just spent together.

Harry was another fifteen minutes into his run when he pulled up hard, pulled the headphones from his ears and spun on his heels.

His gaze met nothing but shrubs and trees and the uneven mud track that he had just been running along. He had felt sure that he had seen a flicker of movement in the trees to his left as he had been running past. Stopping, he paused his music player, feeling certain that he had heard a sound from beyond the edge of the woods. Perhaps the snap of a twig as someone moved out of sight? An unseen observer keeping tabs on his every move or a creature of the woods foraging?

Harry cursed his absurd childish panic under his breath. It was foolish of course; who the hell would be out here keeping tabs on him, especially at this hour of the day?

Teach you for watching all those late night horrors as a kid! he thought, listening once more and this time hearing nothing.

His heart was racing ten to the dozen and he suddenly felt extremely exposed and alone, susceptible to anything that wanted to hunt him down.

He took a deep breath, and then continued on his run. It wasn't long before he would reach the wooden gate that would lead back towards the main high street and home.

It was half an hour later after returning home and having taken a long, hot shower that Harry thought about Maggie Dean, his mind back on the job.

He stood in his kitchen and gazed around at the heart of the house that felt anything but. He looked at the new oven that had hardly been used, at kitchen utensils that were as shiny as the day he had purchased them, and the kitchen table that could happily seat six but was only ever set for one.

His rose tinted glasses had demisted, he was seeing things as they were once more.

And something bothered him.

What was Maggie Dean planning? And what could he do to stop her?

In that instant he made up his mind.

He would go and meet with Natalie later and over a couple of drinks he would persuade her to involve the police. Stifling a yawn, Harry rubbed his eyes. The excesses of the night before and the early morning run were catching up with him, tiredness was creeping in. Normally he would work through the sluggishness, which is what he had had in mind.

He looked at the pile of papers he had arranged on the desk along with the recently made mug of coffee, the steam rising in swirls above the cup. From the lounge came the sound of Neil Young as he started *A Man Needs A Maid*. But it was the stairs that caught his eye, summoning him forward like a moth to a light.

Leaving the folk rock legend to sing to an empty room, the coffee to cool to cold and the papers to remain unread, Harry climbed the stairs to his normally unused bedroom.

Without pulling aside the covers, Harry lay down and closed his eyes.

For the first time in a long while he slept a dreamless sleep, in his bed instead of the chair.

Chapter 32

George Soderman lay in his bed bored and annoyed. He had completed the crossword puzzles in both of the newspapers that the nurse had brought in plus the one in the back of one of those Godforsaken celebrity magazines that had been left lying around. He was annoyed because he had had no word as yet from Harry Stone, and despite the fact that it was part way through Sunday afternoon, a time when most people did not work, he had come to rely on the investigators frequent updates.

Did that mean something had happened to Natalie? Worry suddenly beading his brow with creases of a frown.

He knew that Natalie had promised to visit today; he just hoped that it was sooner rather than later before true paranoia set in. He leant forward and pulled the copy of the newspaper closer to him, not feeling any inclination for a mid morning sleep. He flicked absently through, depressed at the constant stream of violence and murder, both nationally and around the world. Earthquakes here and revolutions there, leaders being forced from power by mass groups of despondent nations as the rest of the Western world watched on with a ripple of unease.

He thought of his baby girl the way she had been the day Mary and he had collected her.

His thoughts acted like a video reel of home movies charting the arrival of the tightly wrapped bundle of smiles and innocence, through those tentative days of newly found parenthood, the first days of school, the friends who had come and gone, teaching her to drive, throwing parties for eighteen and twenty-first birthdays. So many good times, so many lovely times but always with that spectre of unease lurking in the background, that unspoken question that neither Mary or himself wanted to answer, *would Natalie's real parents or family come looking for her, would Natalie want to know her true bloodline?*

George Soderman also thought about the promises he had made to her on the first night they had brought her home. He had leant in close to the crib where she had spent those precious months. He recalled speaking in a soft tone, but the words heartfelt and solemn. He would never let anyone hurt her, and he would always be there for her, no matter what.

Of course he knew that the last promise was wrong on so many levels. He would not be around forever, he was not immortal, and that baton would be passed on to someone else. Over time he had hoped that she would meet a man and settle down, that she would have someone to watch over her when he no longer could.

Perhaps that moment had come.

He wasn't young anymore.

He couldn't square up for a fight, especially when fighting these days was anything but fair.

George's thoughts returned to Harry Stone.

At that moment he heard the sound of voices and laughter followed quickly by the rapid footsteps that eventually brought Natalie through his door and to the side of his bed alongside a huge wave of relief.

He beamed at her, enveloped her in his arms and hugged her tight as if never wanting to let go.

'How are you feeling?' she asked, sitting down on the edge of the bed. The room filled with the scent of her shower gel as the gloom of the world's trouble was deftly pushed aside for a few precious moments. He thought she looked tired, but then again, he was hardly surprised. She had gone through so much in the last few days.

'Much better now,' he replied, clasping hold of her hand, refusing to let go. With Natalie sitting on the edge of his bed, they spoke about everything except the deadly virus that had infiltrated their lives, Maggie Dean.

Her father asked if she had heard or seen Harry Stone. He noted the deep reddish colour that burnt her features and the way she averted eye contact when she spoke. Soderman didn't say anything, but he felt a mixture of a smile and a grimace fighting it out for an appearance over his face.

'What have you got planned for the rest of the day?' he asked, matter-of-factly, closing the page of the paper in front of him.

'Thought I might take a walk into town, maybe go for a drink in the Arms or maybe the George,' she said, again the blush and the avoidance of the eyes telling him everything he needed to know.

When it came time to leave Natalie gave him a hug and planted a kiss on his cheek, the stubble tickling her skin.

'Nat,' her father began, taking her hand and preventing her from moving away.

'What's up?'

'Apart from being in here and aside from Maggie Dean's vendetta against my family?'

'Yeah, apart from that.'

'You know you don't have to visit this evening, enjoy yourself, meet up with some of your friends.'

'Honestly I don't mind,' she replied, sitting back down on the side of the bed.

'Please, just enjoy yourself, but promise me one thing?'

'What's that?'

'Keep your mobile with you at all times and make sure you have Harry Stone's number programmed into your phone?'

Soderman felt the slightest hint of a smile, but it was gone in a flash.

'I promise,' she replied, kissing him once more before leaving the room.

As George Soderman watched his daughter leave, he felt a pang of guilt mingled with a sense of concern edged with a smile.

He just hoped Harry knew what he was doing. More to the point, he hoped that Harry was keeping his eyes peeled for Maggie Dean; the woman was up to something, was planning something and he didn't like the sudden radio silence.

It was as though this was the calm before the storm.

Chapter 33

Robbie Drake opened his eyes.

His vision was hazy and blurred, unclear and distorted in places as shapes danced in front of his eyes as they gradually became distinct, revealing themselves to the man who found himself tied to the bed in the room where he had spent last night with Maggie Dean.

His hands were tied behind his head, his legs shackled at the ankles and spread apart. The bed cover that had been thrown over him was thin and allowed the cold to bite against his skin.

The heavy curtains were pulled all the way across adding to the general dimness of the room. On the bedside table he could just make out the time that was showing as 11:30am. He couldn't recall what time they had fallen asleep; in fact, most of last night had been a muddled and somewhat cloudy affair.

The scent of Maggie's perfume still lingered in the bedroom.

A smile stretched across his face as he recalled the touch of her body against his and of the way she had almost savagely overwhelmed him with her insatiable desire to have all of him.

Her appetite for his sex was almost as incessant and unrelenting as her energy and vigour. Whilst she had mounted him, sitting astride his groin, she had bent down and run her tongue over his flesh, taking little bites of his skin here and there, causing him to gasp out with a mixture of pleasure, excitement and fleeting pain.

When finally she had been satisfied she had surprised him by cuddling up against his hot and weary body. She had rested her head against his chest and fallen asleep. It was the first time that Drake had seen her looking at ease, dare he say normal, the wild look in her eyes for the moment looking to be have been tamed, even for just a short while. Or at least that was what he had thought.

She had woken a little while later and they had moved through to the bedroom where her frantic love making began once more.

The smile faded as his body broke out in goose bumps.

The curtains rippled as he heard a sound from outside the bedroom.

He moved his wrists, trying to recall at what point he had agreed to being tied to the bed.

Not that he was worried; he was enjoying the continued game, salivating at the prospect of more of the same from the woman he had fallen head over heels for and for whom he would do anything she asked.

He looked down at the covers and smiled at the raised sheet near his groin.

He heard movement again and this time the bedroom door opened.

Maggie Dean stood in the doorway, leaning against the frame.

Her slender frame was silhouetted by the brightness of the hallway.

Her hair was pulled back in a ponytail and she wore a tee shirt that she had found in one of the drawers. It came down to the tops of her milky white thighs revealing a small patch of material that was her underwear.

Drake bit his lip in anticipation.

In her right hand she held a tumbler and in her left a bottle of near finished Whisky that they had abused long into the early hours.

'Ready?' she asked her tone playful and her eyes twinkling with mischievousness.

* * *

Maggie made her way to the bed, pausing only to pour a large measure of Bourbon into the glass. She hadn't planned to stay this long; in fact, she hadn't planned to stay the night but Drake had surprised her.

Admittedly he didn't have her voracious near ravenous sexual appetite, likewise he lacked her endurance, but he made up for it in familiarity and understanding of what she craved, what she needed.

Deciding that perhaps he hadn't outstayed his welcome just yet, Maggie screwed the lid back on the bottle of Bourbon and turned to face the man who was tied to the bed.

She had made no arrangements for the day and that in itself was part of her plan. She had wanted a day to collect herself, to gather her mind and her body in readiness for the execution of the final part of her plan.

Reaching the bed she bent down and offered the glass to her play thing, to her toy.

He drank thirstily.

Removing the glass, Maggie drained the final remnants of the amber liquid before letting the glass fall into the folds of the bed covers. She climbed onto the bed, pulled back the covers and, with a giggle of playfulness, leant into Drake and pressed her lips hungrily to his. Drake let out a moan of delirium as she moved down his body, nibbling at his goose flesh prickled skin, gripping his manhood in her tight grip.

Until she was ready to finish with her toy he was hers to have fun with and that was what she intended to do. Her game, her rules, it had always been that way, it always would be that way.

Chapter 34

The day had turned out better than the weather forecasters had reported in the early morning news. The grey skies had lifted and the rain departed; in its place was a blue sky with a scattering of cloud cover that occasionally stole the warmth and left a biting wind.

Harry Stone had been true to his word and had called Natalie; they chatted easily on the phone for a while before agreeing to meet in a pub close to the Soderman residence. And at just before three o'clock that afternoon Harry drove out to The George pub and restaurant that was located on Woodland Road. He parked the car and entered the near empty bar, ordered a pint of Guinness and waited at the bar. Whilst the barman poured the dark liquid Harry took a copy of a Sunday newspaper that had been left on the bar and flicked absently through it.

He had been reading the dismissal report of Arsenal's latest effort to close the gap on the red half of Manchester when the doors opened, followed swiftly by an icy gust of wind. Harry turned and smiled at the woman with the dark hair who had entered carrying with her a small overnight bag. He did a double-take; thinking that it was Natalie, such was the similarity, save for the style and way the woman wore her hair. She returned the smile before disappearing to the opposite end of the bar and settled into a seat, her attention stolen by the barman, their familiarity evident. Perhaps she worked here or was dating the barman or maybe just a patron, Harry thought as he returned his eyes to the dismal football report.

After reading a few more lines that did little to improve his optimism of the forthcoming European tie, he closed the paper and began reading from the front.

'Fancy seeing you here,' said the voice close to his left side. Harry had been so absorbed in reading an article about a recently deceased movie legend that he hadn't heard the door swing open and Natalie walk in.

He turned to greet her, planting a kiss instinctively to her cheek whilst enjoying the smell of her perfume that engulfed him.

'What you drinking?' he asked.

'Medium white if they've got one; I'll go and grab a table.' Harry turned, caught sight of the barman and ordered her drink whilst watching Natalie. Quite simply, she looked beautiful, he thought, smiling to himself as the barman placed her drink in front of Harry and took the money. Harry carried the two drinks over to a table that looked out over the rear of the pub. Natalie had removed her red coat and was hanging it over the back of the chair. She was dressed in a pair of black trousers and a red sweater, her hair pulled back in a ponytail. She sat down on the bench with the padded scarlet cushion, Harry joining her by her side.

'Thanks,' she said, gently tapping her glass against his.

'How was your dad?' Harry asked.

'He looked a little tired but cranky, which means he is getting back to his old self,' she laughed as she added the last part of the sentence and Harry once against felt a smile crease his lips. 'What about you, what did you get up to when you left this morning?'

Harry went through the story of his day, which didn't amount to very much. In the back of his mind he kept asking himself how he was going to approach the subject of getting Natalie to go to the police, and the last thing he wanted to do was to upset her and push her away, just when they were getting so close. The conversation shifted between last night and the past.

Natalie was intrigued with his newly built home and even more so about its past.

'Don't you ever hear strange noises that go bump in the night, or things moving out of the corner of your eye?' she giggled, leaning in close and speaking in a mock whispery voice.

'There's nothing left of the original building as it happens, the fire was so intense that the shell that was left had to be taken down.'

'Do you know what happened?'

'Only what the locals tell me.' He took a sip of his drink and was aware of Natalie intensely gazing at him. He put his drink down, laughed and turned in his seat to face her, their legs brushing against one another.

'Well?'

'God you're like an excited child at Christmas.'

'Hey!' she said, slapping his arm playfully. 'You wait until you see what I am really like at Christmas.' A silence fell between them as the relevance of the words spoken gained momentum in one another minds. It had been such a long time since Harry had been with a girlfriend at Christmas that he had forgotten what it felt like. He briefly thought of Sara and the festive times they had spent together, he smiled and looked across at Natalie, wondering if at the end of the year they would be together or whether their current liaison was perhaps more to do with situation rather than anything of longevity.

'Well?' Natalie pressed, taking a sip of her drink which was close to half empty.

'Nothing sinister, the elderly owners must have built a fire the night before and, according to the fire report a log looks to have fallen from the grate and started the fire.'

'What about the couple?'

'They weren't so lucky.'

'Oh, that is so sad,' she said, lowering her eyes for a moment, taking a sip of her drink. 'I'd love to see what you have done with the place sometime?' she said finally, lifting the mood.

'Well I think I probably owe you a dinner.'

'What about tomorrow night?'

'You don't hold back do you?' Harry said, finishing his drink and laughing, not able to recall the last time he had been out with a woman who had made him laugh and smile so much and at the same time make him feel so at ease. He supposed Sara had when they had first started dating, but as the relationship built the cracks had started early on, the smiles had then given way and became lost to the quarrels.

'Blame it on my father; he always told me I should just go out and get what I want, not to hold back or lose out.'

'And what is it that you want?' Natalie smiled and gave a low chuckle before looking more serious.

'This whole nightmare to be over with, that's what I want.' she said and for the merest of moments she looked more vulnerable and fragile than ever. 'Can I get you another one?' she asked, emptying her drink and nodding in the direction of his depleted glass.

'Thanks.' Harry watched as Natalie walked towards the bar, the black trousers clinging tight to her rear and against her slender legs, her low heels adding a little height. He felt his face redden as she turned and caught his stare as she rolled her eyes in mock-annoyance before smiling and turning to order both drinks, chatting good naturedly with the barman.

Harry looked past her and gazed around the interior of the bar, taking in the pictures of landscape scenes that adorned the walls and the collection of real ale beer mats that were tacked above the bar. Harry caught sight of the dark haired woman he had seen enter the bar earlier; she had moved away from the bar and was sat at a table a little way back. She seemed lost in the pages of a book whilst drinking from a coffee mug. Harry wondered if maybe she was starting a shift behind the bar soon. He thought of the similarity between the girl and Natalie but realised now it was not a close resemblance. Whilst pale features and hair colour were the same, style and manner were not. He let his eyes return to Natalie at the bar, watching her with a smile and real notion that maybe, just maybe, things might turn out okay between them.

'So what do you say?' Natalie said after returning from the bar.

'About what?' Harry asked, genuinely looking, and feeling, as though he had missed something in a prior conversation.

'About coming over to yours for something to eat tomorrow night?'

'Sure why not, how about I pick you up?'

'Are you sure?'

'Course, what time.'

'How about seven-ish?'

'It's a date.' Harry said, only realising afterwards what he had said and what the implications were. He turned to look at Natalie who had averted her eyes, her face caught in mid-blush.

As dinner plans were made the dark haired patron finished her coffee and left the bar. Neither Harry nor Natalie gave the woman a second glance.

Chapter 35

Maggie Dean stood outside the pub and took a deep lungful of air. She felt hot in the dark hair piece and felt a cackle of laughter waiting to escape but she did her best to suppress the urge.

She had watched the couple for the past hour.

The more she watched them, the more she felt her anger rising. Especially towards Natalie. Her sister had laughed and smiled and joked as though she had no other care in the world. Maggie smiled; it wouldn't be long before her sister would have nothing further to smile about.

Feeling that itch of anger that was in need of scratching, Maggie left the entrance to the pub and walked the short distance to the area where she had parked her car, not far from Hayward Way.

As she reached the car she heard footsteps.

She looked up.

Drake appeared through the trees, his face furrowed and agitated as he spoke in a low voice on his mobile phone. When he reached the car he saw Maggie's quizzical look, and the look of irritation that joined it.

'I thought I told you to stay in the car,' she rebuked, sounding like a mother scolding an errant child.

'Business.' Drake offered by way of an explanation and feeling no desire to offer anything else as they both got back into the car. 'What's up?' he asked, looking across at the woman who sat in the driver's seat and who looked as though her entire world had crumbled. Silence descended over the pair for a few moments; only when they saw another car pull in behind them did Maggie offer a near silent curse. She started the car and pulled out of the parking area, watching as the silver haired owner of the newly arrived car let her dog out from the boot.

'What business?' she asked as they left the village and headed in the direction of Drake's temporary residence.

'Nothing much, just a couple of jobs a mate wants to push my way.'

'Like?'

'Inquisitive aren't you?'

'I like to know what's going on with the men I sleep with,' she replied, a lop-sided grin spreading across her features as she took her hand from the steering wheel and roughly squeezed the top of his thigh.

'Don't you worry, it won't interfere with what you want me to do for you,' he said, looking out of the passenger window, not used to sharing his business dealings with anyone. He had learnt a long time ago that you couldn't trust everyone, especially the people you thought you *could* trust. With Maggie he thought it was different, but even so he still wanted to keep his business his own for the moment.

They drove in silence until they reached Drake's flat.

* * *

Drake and Maggie lay in bed, the room – like the rest of the flat – smelling of stale smoke, sweat and burnt food. Drake was exhausted. As soon as they had returned home she had fallen upon him, dragged him to the bedroom and repeated the previous evening's menu of uninhibited pleasure. The only difference was that today she was more aggressive and less talkative. It was almost as though she was performing a final act before fleeing. Something she resolutely denied.

With her appetite momentarily satisfied, she lay next to him, unmoving, breathing slowly. Her hands roamed his skinny torso, tracing the series of tattoos that adorned his body and that were like his own personal diary of events in a life gone badly.

'So what other business do you do?' she asked again, her voice low and breathless. In the times they had lain in bed before, Maggie had tried to broach the subject of his business deals that kept him with notes in his pocket but each time he shifted the conversation away.

Drake laughed, astonished at the relentlessness of this woman. He knew she was wired differently from any other woman he had ever met; it was a thought that scared him a little and excited him a lot. He gave in to the normal vowel of silence concerning business, what harm could it do, he thought, both his mind and body weary to the onslaught of her questions.

'You could say it is a little bit of import and export, mostly import and distribution.'

'Like what.'

'Usual, Cigarettes, alcohol, drugs.'

'What do you have to do?'

'Collect them from a place out in the woods, actually belongs to the same guy who owns this place. Not that you ever see him, he keeps well out of the way. Then I get told where they need to be driven to and that's pretty much it, simple really.'

'Where's this place in the woods that you have to drive to?'

'Not far. Mind you it is a bloody eerie place; the place is surrounded by woods, pure Stephen King territory that's for sure. Bloody hate going out there, especially if it's dark.'

'Does that mean your phone call earlier was about a forthcoming job?'

'Yep!'

'When?'

'Maybe later this evening, not sure yet just waiting for the call.'

'Can I come along?' Drake was hesitant at first, but then relaxed. Hell, it might be fun having someone along instead of driving out to the old farm alone. He hated the place anyway.

'Sure, why not.'

Maggie fell silent, closing her eyes for a moment. Her plans were revising once more.

As early afternoon gave way to early evening, Maggie Dean left Drake sleeping whilst she went through to what passed as the kitchen and lit a cigarette. Her stomach was growling, hungry and in need of sustenance.

Maggie ignored the pangs of hunger and smoked another cigarette as soon as she had finished the first, starter and main course now taken care of. Her hunger abating for the moment, she was smiling in that way she did when things were beginning to come together.

Her entire plan had been to creep up to the Soderman house and deal with Natalie there and then; what could be better than for the girl to die in the grounds of the very place that upset Maggie so much? A place that was the epitome of what she herself did not have, a nice place to live, a loving family, stability and, to make matters worse, a happy life at that.

But things had become complicated.

The investigator had seen to that. He had arranged for the locks to be changed, and that very same investigator was now hanging around like a bad smell. It wouldn't be so easy to get Natalie alone now; it was a problem she had to deal with, a problem that could be fixed by playing a card that had already been stacked in the deck.

If her plan was to work then Harry Stone would have to be dealt with and she knew exactly what to do about that, and thanks to Drake and his lapse mouth, not to mention his phobia of remote buildings and dark woods, she now had the perfect location for her plan to be carried out.

She sauntered back to the doorway of the bedroom where she watched Drake sleep, an unseen observer. It was time for her plans to be moved forward; it was time for Maggie Dean to finish what she had started.

Chapter 36

Harry dropped Natalie off at the entrance to the hospital, said goodnight and planted a kiss on her cheek as he walked her to the doorway. Under the light of the automatic doors his kiss was reciprocated as she wrapped her arms around him, her red coat billowing in the wind that had crept up on them during the afternoon.

'Thanks for a lovely afternoon,' she said, pulling away and buttoning her coat.

'So I'll pick you up tomorrow night yeah?' Harry confirmed, leaning in to her and arranging her collar that was caught slightly.

'As long as you don't mind, I can always catch a taxi or the bus.'

'No that's fine.'

'Okay, till tomorrow then.'

'Tomorrow it is, and remember, ring me if you need anything.' Natalie turned and walked through the automatic doors. 'Say hi to your dad for me,' he uttered but she had been swallowed up by the movement of patients, nurses and visitors and within seconds she was gone. Left in its place was the lingering smell of her perfume and the touch of her hand that had been clasped to his.

He had enjoyed the afternoon.

They had ended up eating in the pub before taking a walk along the path that led to the village green where they had sat, talked and watched as parents tried to keep up with their energetic children as they played and ran and screamed with delight, their bodies oblivious to the rapidly changing weather.

During moments of silence that had fallen between them, they both became lost to their own thoughts. The silence was not awkward or uncomfortable in any way. Neither Harry nor Natalie felt as though words were needed. Harry had looked at the kids running around and wondered, briefly, if children lay in the future for him. Would he be one of those harried and tired looking parents in years to come chasing after a son or daughter? Surprisingly the thought did little to worry him, instead he felt a tinge of a smile, a hope that he would someday have children of his own.

This was all alien territory for Harry; most of his weekends were spent at the office or at the very least by himself. Yet today was different and today he was seeing just what he had missed for so long. If Harry was honest he would have enjoyed spending the evening with Natalie such was the closeness that they had formed. But he also knew she had to see her father, that she had other things to deal with and that he himself was her protector. He had made that promise to George.

He had failed in his bid to convince Natalie to go to the police, at least for the moment at any rate. They had discussed it but she had mooted the point, but did agree that if anything else happened then she would consider it more seriously.

He wondered again for what seemed like the hundredth time whether or not he should put a call in to his friend on the force, but thought better of it. At this moment he didn't want to alienate Natalie or George, more so Natalie.

Returning to the car Harry drove away from the hospital.

He had promised to swing by the Soderman home and check to make sure that everything was okay, and then he was heading home. It was only later that he realised he had referred to his house as home; it was the first time he had done so and yet it was such a huge deal.

* * *

Later that evening, after calling in at the Soderman's house and finding nothing amiss, Harry had called into the supermarket on the high street not far from Natalie's childhood home and purchased a few items that may have been construed as shopping, something he rarely did. Happy with his purchases of milk, bread, cheese and a pack of bacon plus a carton of eight small bottles of French beer, he headed home in a positive mood, a smile etched over his lips.

Sitting in his reading chair later in the evening, having finished off several bottles of beer and having eaten two bacon sandwiches whilst listening to a Neil Young's *Chrome Dreams II* CD back to back, Harry felt the overriding urge to sleep. Another feeling that was alien to his normal routine.

As he had done earlier in the day he climbed the stairs to his bedroom, this time actually pulling aside the covers and sliding beneath.

As his eyelids began to close and his body ceased its battle with fatigue, he wondered what tomorrow would bring. He wondered if finally he would be able to locate Maggie Dean and put an end to Natalie and George Soderman's ordeal.

If, at that point, he would have had any inkling what the next day had in store for him or the others, he would most likely have driven to Natalie's side, despite the tiredness, and protected her like he should have done in the first place. He would never have left her alone at the hospital; he would in fact never have left her side, and he most certainly would not have left her alone at her house, new locks or no new locks.

Chapter 37

The train that pulled into London Waterloo at just gone 10am was packed as all London trains were. As soon as the doors were open the heaving mass of bodies surged from every exit and battled their way firstly through the ticket barriers and then out onto the concourse that was, simply put, madness.

Harry pushed his way through the ticket barrier, doing his best to ignore the constant shoving and moaning that surrounded him. He decided to head for a coffee stand and quickly ordered a coffee and toasted cheese and ham sandwich to go. His stomach had been groaning the entire length of the journey and his hopes of grabbing an overpriced and unexciting sandwich and coffee on the train had diminished the further into the journey he had got.

Taking his delayed breakfast to a row of plastic seats Harry sat down and took a bite of his food as he watched the mass of bodies rush by.

He had caught the 8:30am train having only been in the office for little over an hour.

He had awoken shortly after 6am, rejuvenated and re-energized by his sleep, and ready to get back to his day job.

After a brief conversation with Natalie shortly before 7:30am, he headed for work.

On his own, surrounded by silence save for the sound of the coffee pot that was bubbling away, Harry went through the paperwork and caught up on some email messages.

It wasn't until just before 8am that his day changed from easy saunter to complete chaos.

He had checked his emails and the answer phone and had found several messages from his newest client, Margaret Mayhew. After each email or message she became more and more frantic, as though she was slowly but surely cracking up before him, hysterical in the end.

Despite the lack of tears in the phone messages, Harry thought that they probably weren't far from a deluge.

And then she rang.

She was in a state.

She had had enough. Wanted to have it out with her husband, would not be cheated on for one second longer, it had to end and end now. She ranted, almost to the point that Harry wondered if taking her case on had been a mistake. After all, most of his cases were missing persons and those who employed him were thankful that someone was willing to take up the search that the police had long since given up on.

She offered to double the fee if he could get proof of his infidelity so that she could start the divorce proceedings, at which point she hung up.

Harry had made a mug of coffee and was trying to calm himself down when the phone rang again. It was the same lady; although this time she was a lot calmer than before. He wanted to say cold, but maybe it was just that she was resigned to what was going on, and what needed to happen now.

She apologised for her outburst, blaming the tirade on lack of sleep and mental torture. At which point the investigator wondered if she was maybe just a little dramatic.

Margaret Mayhew was unrepentant in her offer to pay double the investigator's fee if the matter could be resolved quickly. She gave Harry a list of her husband's movements for the day; apparently he had been in London since Saturday evening and was due back Tuesday.

At that point Harry Stone's day was set.

He had quickly checked the train times and then after typing a quick email to his assistant he left the office and headed for the train station with a print out of the Mayhew file and picture of the husband in his brown case. With a bit of luck he wouldn't be long and could get back before the early afternoon gave way to evening. He was picking Natalie up at 7pm and she had his number if she needed him; also Natalie was due to be with her father at the hospital for a while, a safe haven away from harm, he hoped.

Finishing his breakfast, his mouth now heavy with the thick and syrupy liquid, Harry made his way out of the station, down the escalators and across to the bus terminal.

Whilst he waited for his connection, his eyes watched the series of buses that drove by, the throng of everyday life and the mixture of humanity that swept passed him.

He looked to his left, knowing that that was the direction in which he would be heading. He thought for a moment about taking the walk over London Bridge but decided that time was against him; today he wanted to get the information he needed and get back. Nothing more and nothing less. He wanted this Mayhew client out from under his feet and if he could get a double fee out of it then so be it.

Despite the sudden rush of business to the day, he was already looking forward to seeing Natalie this evening and not even a diversion to the City could change that.

As the bus rumbled into the stop he smiled as he pushed his way through the doors and found a seat and a newspaper that had been left. As the bus trundled along its route, Harry Stone lost himself in the pages of the newspaper.

Chapter 38

Drake had not been lying when he had told Maggie that the remote and dilapidated farmhouse was only a short drive out of town. After only twenty minutes drive they arrived at a gravel track whose entrance was overgrown with skeletal branches. It was a gravel track that could so easily have been missed if you didn't know it was there. The driver pulled in and drove slowly through the avenue of trees that hung over the van and blocked out the sunlight like a canopy of marauding arms.

After a few moments he stopped the van, put it in idle and jumped out. Ahead was a gate that had seen better days, paint was falling off in clumps and it looked as though one good shove would render it broken.

Drake ushered the gate back and then returned to drive the van through.

More of the same followed trees that obstructed the sun's rays and made Maggie thankful that she had brought her jacket with her. In the passenger's seat she rubbed her hands up and down her arms in order to banish the cold that was seeping through to her skin. The chill of the location and the thrill of the find were both exciting yet made her somewhat apprehensive.

Finally they drove out into the open and Maggie Dean could not do anything about the location but smile as she saw what presented itself to her. Quite simply put, it was perfect for what she wanted.

Eager to look around, Maggie jumped out of the van even before Drake had brought his vehicle to a halt.

Like an excited schoolgirl on the last day of term, she raced across the final expanse of rugged terrain, delighting in the silence that greeted her ears and the absolute remoteness that met her gaze. Finally she stood in front of the run down farmhouse whilst to her left were a series of out buildings. She said nothing just bit her lip a little, doing her best to contain the anticipation that was building within. The cold was now gone, replaced by a new sensation.

Behind her appeared Drake, a smug look etched over his features.

'Do you like?' he asked, not needing an answer, the look on her face enough of a response.

'What time will you have finished your business?' she asked, not taking her eyes from the property, transfixed and hypnotized by the place.

'Late afternoon, why?'

'I've got one final task for you to do for me.'

'Maggie…' Drake began but was cut short quickly.

'Trust me Drake, this is the last thing I will ask of you, and look at it this way, come this time tomorrow all this will be over and me and you will be out of here.'

'Together?'

'Together.'

Drake came up behind the woman who both fascinated and frightened him at times. He wrapped his arms tightly around her waist and nestled his face into her neck, kissing her delicate pale skin. She tilted her head to the side, let him lavish his kisses upon her flesh, ignored the roaming hands that disappeared beneath her coat and under her jumper as actions of a condemned man.

Maggie Dean was in a different place; her thoughts were running on an entirely different plane with plans that did not include Robbie Drake, despite her promises.

She giggled, feeling his excitement grow and press into her rear. But her laughter was more directed at him. Men were so stupid, so easy to navigate, so unproblematic when it came to wanting to control them.

She pulled free from his arms and saw the desperate plea etched over his face, the look of disappointment that remained there.

She gripped his chin with her right hand, squeezing his pallid features with thumb and first finger.

'No time now soldier, we've got work to do. Later!' With that she released him and playfully tapped the front of his trousers which were now tighter than before. She left him standing, mouth agape, as she walked towards the playground that would be Natalie Soderman's final resting place.

Chapter 39

Natalie Soderman entered the hospital, thrusting her mobile phone back in to her pocket, having just left the second message on Harry's answer phone. She needed to speak with him, had to speak with him, and now was not the time for him to be playing hide and seek.

Carrying the day's newspapers which were tucked beneath her arm and a takeaway coffee she had bought whilst waiting for her connecting bus in town warming her hands.

Despite the blue almost cloudless skies outside, a biting chill was nipping at her skin as she walked those now well known steps through the reception area with the cafeteria on her right, followed by the charity shop displaying second-hand wares such as paperback books, DVDs, puzzles and VHS videos before passing the newspaper kiosk, flower stall and the row of hardly used payphones.

She was tired.

She hadn't slept well last night, if at all, and despite the bravado she had shown to Harry yesterday afternoon, she had wished upon nothing else that he had been with her last night for varying reasons. At one point she had even considered ringing him but at the last moment decided against it.

Every sound that had reached her ears made her heart rate increase and her breathing become laboured and awkward as cold beads of sweat raised goose bumps over her skin. Several times she had thrown the covers from her bed and padded slowly to the bedroom door and stood listening as though she were an eavesdropping child trying to hear what her parents were saying.

Each time she heard nothing and would return to bed, pulled the covers to her chin and closed her eyes in the hope that sleep would come. It never did.

With both her bedside table lamp and the hallway light left on in an effort to banish the enemy of her nightmares, Natalie had listened to the sound of the house settling, wondering for the umpteenth time if maybe, just maybe, Maggie Dean, her estranged sister, had finally found her once more. If maybe she was somewhere close by waiting to strike, or was she even inside of the house despite the change of locks? That thought alone had brought a fresh wave of paranoia to the party.

Every other sound she heard she convinced herself that the delusional woman had somehow managed to get into the house, despite the new locks, and was, in that instant, creeping up the stairs to exact a revenge Natalie should not and could not understand.

All her life she had wondered what it would have been like to have a brother or a sister, to enjoy the games and the amusement that having siblings brought. But those thoughts had been lost indefinitely, banished by a sister she had never known and who had developed a vendetta against her. And for what reason? Was she jealous? Did she hate the life her sister had and the life she did not?

At 6am Natalie had given up the fight and had thrown the covers off in agitation and annoyance. She showered, with the door locked and the wicker chair pushed against its frame. She dressed in her room with the door closed and locked, dressing in a pair of dark jeans and a black sweater and a pair of white sneakers, perfect for running she thought with dark humour to mask her fear.

Downstairs she had made a quick breakfast of toast and jam and a pot of coffee.

Having failed to banish her worries with the radio and the television, Natalie had simply given up and went through to her father's study.

For a while she simply sat there in her father's chair and stared at the mass of books that he had collected over a lifetime. The volumes were both hardback and paperback, a mixture of textbooks for study; medical, literature guides and biographies, historical events as well as his fictional guilty pleasures mingled in with the classics of Charles Dickens, Thomas Hardy, William Shakespeare and Lewis Carroll as well as Daphne Du Maurier and Agatha Christie.

Her eyes had lowered to the various shelves that had been erected around the room. All of them displaying a varying array of keepsakes and pictures set in gold and silver frames.

When the coffee pot had beeped its readiness, Natalie had poured herself a large mug and then called Harry on his mobile. He had sounded alert and awake; she wondered how much sleep he had had and what time he had woken up. She also wondered if he had wanted to be with her last night instead of on his own.

After the phone call she had returned to the study, affectionately glancing over some of the pictures that charted her family life before, during and after the death of her mother and the arrival of herself.

It was as she looked at a sepia image of her mother and father on their wedding day that a thought popped into her mind like a bullet from a gun.

She hurried quickly across to the table and pulled open the folder of her fathers that contained all the info on Maggie Dean and Harry Stone's investigation.

Natalie flicked through the pages and found what she was after.

She held the grainy image in front of her face and felt the cold hand of terror brush against her flesh.

The dark haired woman in the George, the one sitting firstly at the bar before taking a table to the side, the one she had smiled at when ordering the drinks.

Maggie Dean.

Natalie had felt her body wane on her feet as though she could collapse in a faint.

Leaning forward to steady herself against the table she took a deep breath and then looked up at the gaping windows of the study.

Was anyone out there?

Was *she* there, watching her, waiting?

Waiting for what? What was she planning?

It had taken Natalie a while to calm herself, to check the doors and windows but calm herself she had.

Now, several hours later, Natalie entered her father's ward, hoping to be able to sneak a visit out of hours. She needed to be someplace other than home. Without being able to contact Harry and with her father in hospital she felt more alone now than ever.

Ahead of her walked one of the nurses who she had come to know fairly well.

'Natalie.' The nurse said, surprised to see her. 'What are you doing here?'

'I was hoping to sneak a visit with my father, what do you think to the chances?' she asked, her face looking sheepish and uncomfortable at asking. The nurse smiled and looked behind her.

'I can't let you see him; he is having his examination, what about going for a coffee and then coming back?' The nurse saw the visible signs of deflation cross the daughter's face. 'I'm sorry Natalie; I wish I could but…'

'No that's fine honestly; I didn't think I would be able to see him.'

'Are you okay? You looked tired.'

'Sleepless night last night that's all.'

'Tell you what, why don't you give me those papers and I'll take them in to him; come back in half an hour when the doctor has finished his rounds and I'll see what I can do.'

Natalie thanked the nurse and handed over the papers.

As she edged away from the ward, from the sanctuary of people, she felt a sense of unease. She looked around at everyone who walked past her, trusting no one.

Instead of heading into the cafeteria she walked out of the front of the hospital and pulled out her phone and tried to contact Harry once more.

Chapter 40

Harry stood on the opposite side of the road from where his target was currently located. Margaret Mayhew's husband was speaking with an Asian man whilst buying fresh fruit from the man's market stall. Harry checked the picture as supplied from his client once more and compared it against the live version that stood across the road.

In his time as an investigator he had seen *and* investigated all manner of people and he was constantly surprised by the fact that it was those who didn't fit the bill, the image in his head who were the ones who cheated or abused their spouses et cetera. Looking at the man buying fruit across the road Harry couldn't say for definite but he most certainly didn't fit the bill of a free spirited gigolo that his wife had painted her husband to be.

Heading for the pedestrian crossing, Harry waited for the lights to change, not wanting to take a chance with the lunacy that was London traffic, albeit taxis, buses or crazy drivers.

His target, Derek Mayhew, shared a joke with the man, handed across money and then took his purchases and walked down the street still enjoying the joke the men had shared with one another. With the lights having finally changed Harry fell in step and followed the man.

In his pocket his phone rang but Harry didn't hear, he had earlier changed the ring tone profile to silent thinking he would feel the vibration of the device.

Above him the skies that had been blue on his arrival in the capital had now changed to a charcoal grey and held the definite threat of rain.

Pulling his coat tight against his body in an effort to block the coldness, he silently followed.

Chapter 41

Robbie Drake had been quicker than expected in completing his delivery. When he got back to the flat he found Maggie stretched out on the bed, her eyes closed and her body wrapped within the covers. He thought about undressing and joining her for a little afternoon fun but she had asked him to wake her up when he got back and not wanting to ruin the mood that was currently between them he followed instructions.

'What time is it?' she asked drowsily, wiping the sleep from the corner of her eyes.

'Just gone 2pm' he said, enjoying the view of her as she threw the covers back and clambered out of bed. She made her way to the window and pulled the curtains apart. A light splatter of rain covered the glass and the skies looked darker than when she had fallen asleep.

'Ready?' he asked, excited to be able to help her, knowing that this time tomorrow the Sodermans would be history and they could move on, begin their life together.

'Yep! Just need to get dressed and then all set for the party to begin.'

'Where do you want to go first?'

'Back out to the farmhouse, want to make sure everything is set.'

'Babe it is, I promise you. Checked, double and triple checked. I did it before coming back here.'

'It doesn't hurt to check again,' she replied calmly, not wanting to bite. She reached up and touched his face with her hands before brushing her lips to his face.

* * *

Drake pulled up to the farmhouse, trying to push aside the personal demons that always came with a visit to this place. Maggie climbed out of the van and made her way to the entrance. In the silhouette of the darkening sky and with the rain falling, this place looked like something out of a Hollywood horror movie, a Bela Lugosi or a Christopher Lee Friday night special.

'Okay, can you show me where we are going to take her?' Maggie asked, following Drake as he pushed his way through the damaged front gate and around to the side of the property.

At the side of the farmhouse was a collection of out-buildings that at one time or another had most likely been used to store feed for the animals and housed the animals themselves. The buildings still looked sturdy; the brickwork intact and winning its battle against the elements of time.

Drake unlocked the only building that still had a complete door attached.

As soon as the door was opened the smell of damp hit them both. They entered.

Drake switched on the overhead strip light that had been fixed a while back. The single cylinder did its best to dispel the darkness but the outer corners of the room were still hidden by an almost inky blackness.

The room was empty save for a few discarded boxes which were now empty and lay strewn about in various places around the room. In the corner was a small box of tea-light candles that had been opened. Drake explained that they had been left over from before the light above had been fitted. He joked that they were more likely to give off better light than the overhead. Maggie ignored the humour hardly raising a smile, her thoughts were focusing on a use for the room.

The floor was stone and there were no windows.

Drake took his torch from his pocket, switched it on and swept the shaft of light into the far corner. Hidden by the gloom was what Maggie was looking for. A trap door in the floor.

Drake bent down and unlocked the gleaming gold padlock, then lifted the lid.

Below them lay the small space which measured no more than three feet square.

He shone his torch down but the beam couldn't penetrate the gloom. The space was exactly what she needed, exactly the kind of location befitting her plan. A smile spread across her features at the realisation that everything was coming together, that despite the complications which had tried to derail her plan, to complicate matters, everything was on track.

'Perfect!' she said, almost salivating at the prospect. 'We've got a little time before we have to leave, how about you show me the old farmhouse,' Maggie said, playfully rubbing the small of his back.

'I don't know, the building is a little unsafe and besides there's no electricity in there any more.'

'You've got your torch.'

'Yeah but…'

'Besides it will make it much more fun,' she said, reaching around the back of his neck and pulling his face towards her, her tongue sliding effortlessly inside his mouth, probing and enticing, her breath tasting sweet and tantalizing. Drake slipped the torch into his jacket pocket and gripped her tightly in his arms.

Chapter 42

Natalie had just finished her second coffee and was contemplating the vending machine and more significantly the line of chocolate that was goading her into parting with the loose change she knew she had in her purse. Whilst the battle of wits raged in her mind, she heard a friendly voice speak close to her ear. Natalie looked up and saw the nurse she had spoken to earlier smiling down at her.

'Hi!' she said, sitting herself down on the red plastic chair opposite, her hands cradling a Styrofoam cup of coffee and a half eaten sandwich which she quickly placed down upon the table.

'Hi.' Natalie replied wavering between uncertainty and suspicion. 'Is everything okay?' she asked wondering if something was wrong with her father. The nurse saw her concern and quickly eased her worry with a smile and gesture of the hands.

'Your father is fine, at least he was complaining about the food to the doctor so I am guessing that is a good sign.'

Natalie stifled a laugh and fought the urge to cry. She was not normally one for tears and emotional breakdowns in public places, she was more private. But with a lack of sleep last night and the sudden realisation of the predicament she was in, coupled with the appearance of her estranged sister showing up at the very same pub that she herself was drinking in was proving all too much. And especially given the fact that she couldn't get hold of Harry either, her emotional state, she thought, was unravelling before her like a loose thread on a shirt.

All of a sudden the threat was very much real.

Perhaps Harry had been right. Perhaps now was the time to go to the police.

'Thanks,' was all she managed to say, staring down at her empty coffee cup and wishing it was something stronger.

'Well I've got to be back on duty shortly but listen, your father will definitely be ready to leave today. Just waiting for the specialist to give him the all clear which we think he will and then he can get back to normality, albeit with a large dose of "taking it easy".' As the nurse stood up she smiled at the young woman, seeing in her the look of fatigue and weariness that came with having a parent in hospital and the uncertainty that brought with it. With Natalie on her own once more she decided on the coffee refill and another attempt at ringing Harry.

Chapter 43

To say that Harry was bored pretty much amounted to the biggest understatement he could possibly think of. Derek Mayhew, if he was the greatest gigolo since Don Juan, was doing the world's outstanding impression of a very a normal guy. After buying his selection of fruit from the market stall he had laboured slowly down the street finally stopping at a small coffee bar. It was in the same place that Harry now sat, albeit several seats away from the man who had already tucked into a full fry up and was now slurping his way through this third or maybe fourth coffee.

Harry looked down at his file notes again.

It was the correct man.

But something didn't sit right.

Something at the back of his mind was nibbling away leaving only strands of unease dangling in place.

Pulling out his phone he was about to call his assistant when he noticed the missed calls he had on his phone, all from Natalie. He silently cursed himself, before promptly hitting the redial button and waited for the call to connect.

When it did it went straight through to voicemail.

Ending the call Harry dialled the office, deciding to check in with his assistant Val, his heart racing with concern almost as much as annoyance at turning his phone to silent.

She picked up on the second ring.

'Hey Val, Harry here, how's everything going?' he never knew why he asked that, he knew that when he was out of the office, in fact when he was in the office as well come to think of it, that she ran the show. Val Hardy had worked for the senior partner of a five-hundred strong international law firm for close to twenty years prior to being poached by his predecessor, Laurence Hunter.

It was precisely for that reason that the hairs on the back of Harry's neck stood to attention when he heard the uneasiness in his assistant's voice. Part of her facade, as well as knowing his files inside out and not being afraid of his technological changes in recent times, was her utter calmness in times of worry.

Not today though, and that worried Harry.

'I was about to call you,' she said, tripping over her words as she tried to get them out quickly but succinctly.

When she had finished speaking Harry was simply at a loss for words.

He looked down at the file in front of him and then across at the man who was getting up from his seat and making his way to the counter to pay for his food.

'I'm sorry Harry; I should have completed the background check quicker for you but she had all the papers and they all seemed genuine, she seemed authentic.'

'Don't be silly Val, nothing you could have done about this one, she had planned this and planned it well. Shit!' he said more to himself than anyone else but his words were heard.

The man at the payment counter, along with staff and other patrons of the cafe, looked at the investigator with disapproving eyes and unspoken displeasure. Harry looked back apologetically but the damage was done.

'Harry, I don't know who the hell you are trailing but it certainly isn't Derek Mayhew and if it is then he is going to be a very rich man considering he died two years ago.'

'His wife?' Harry asked absently, already packing up the file knowing the truth.

'Never married.'

He laughed, but the sound contained no trace of humour. He slammed the file shut and went to the payment counter.

'Can you find the next train back from Waterloo please Val?'

'Wait a tick.' Whilst his assistant tapped away at the keyboard trying to navigate the train time website, Harry's thoughts turned to Natalie and the batch of missed calls. A new sense of dread was beginning to wrap its icy tendrils around him, and rightly so.

Harry handed across a note in payment for his multiple cups of coffee and then dropped several coins into the tip tin before leaving, happy to be out from under the roof of the cafe he had spent too long in for no good reason.

'How you doing?' he asked, feeling the patter of rain against his face.

'Looks as though they are every quarter past the hour for the next few.'

'Thanks Val, speak later.' With that he ended the call and ran hoping for either a bus or a taxi, whichever came first. As he ran his fingers danced over the keypad of his mobile as he tried to redial Natalie's number.

The phone went straight to voicemail once more as his worry went into overdrive.

Chapter 44

The room was almost dark as Maggie let herself be guided from the makeshift bed by an invisible Robbie Drake who lurked around her in the dark.

As before, their love making had been frantic, heavy, repeated and exhaustive.

When they had finished they lay together, both lost in their own thoughts, and it had been Drake who had fallen silent, asleep.

Maggie had used the time creatively.

In her mind she ran through the order of events as she saw them occurring.

When Drake came to, his mind hazy, they made love again and this time Maggie knew it would be for the last time. Before they had made their way to what would have been a bedroom years ago, Drake had given her the guided tour. To say the farmhouse was a ruin was equalled in its stupidity with the assumption that peace would eventually come to the Middle East. The stone flooring on the ground floor was the only section that looked in good repair. Beams were eaten away by death watch beetles; discarded furniture lay battered and broken along with leftover crockery and empty bottles. Glass was missing from the windows and the stairs to the upper floor were precarious and almost impossible to climb. But climb them they did and Drake continued his guided tour of the upper floor. The upstairs was more or less in the same state as the lower floor. Missing floorboards and shattered glass, unwanted knick-knacks and a chilling breeze that rattled through the upstairs like a silent unseen enemy flowing through the stream of broken windows.

Maggie hadn't realised that she was shivering until Drake appeared at her side and wrapped her tiny frame within his arms and chuckled to himself.

'She's a bit breezy isn't she?' he said, guiding her out of the fractured hallway and into a side room that had once been a bedroom, evidence of a double bed that had seen better days pushed against a wall of peeling paper exposing damp.

Maggie let herself be guided from the bedroom and back along the hallway to the top of the stairs. A small amount of light crept in giving the place an air of gloom; it felt like one of those buildings you always saw in horror films shortly before the group of intrepid out of town types became aware that they were not alone and being pursued by an unseen enemy who lurked close by.

'Give me your hand and I'll guide you,' he said, taking one step forward and checking the step. He swung the beam of his torch down the stairs, checking his path.

It only took a second.

But that was all the time Maggie needed. It was part of her make-up, to plan, to create something from nothing.

Hands apart, the darkness pressing against them, she pushed Drake hard. His surprise and her strength had been enough.

She heard his gasp and fall, a stifled breath of shock before the revelation of truth set in.

The sound of his body crashing down the stairs was ended by the crippling crunch and then silence.

Breathing fast, her body feeling ice cool yet sweltering hot, she reached blindly towards the remnants of the stair rail that she knew was located against the wall – the left hand side banister and rail had long since fallen away to ruin.

She listened intently trying to make out any sound from the fallen man below.

She heard nothing.

For the first time in a long while she was nervous.

Maybe Drake had been right about this remote farmhouse. With its surrounding woodlands and sinister seclusion, it really did feel as though invisible persons were watching you from the edge of the forest ready to strike when you turned your back.

Maggie made her way slowly and carefully down the stairs, reaching the bottom with a sense of relief and achievement at not falling.

She stopped at the base of the stairs and listened again.

Nothing made a noise save for the rustling of the trees outside and the whistling of the wind that rattled through the open, damaged windows.

She crouched down.

She could see Drake's fallen body, unmoving and inert, a static form half shrouded in the semi-darkness of the late afternoon.

Holding her breath she flexed the fingers of each hand and blindly explored the ground around her looking for the torch and hoping that it wasn't broken but fearing the worst.

She found Drake's hand first and gave herself a start.

Branding herself foolish she continued her search and finally located the torch. She flicked the on/off button but got nothing. She ran her fingers over the front of the glass but found no obvious surface cracks. Slamming her balled fist over the top of the device she was amazed to find that it did the job, a beam of light suddenly appeared and lit a section of floor.

Pushing herself to her feet she swept the area around her, the beam coming to rest on Drake.

His eyes were closed and she could detect no breathing.

She crouched closer and checked his pulse, double checking, not wanting any surprises.

Nothing.

Could it really be that simple? She asked herself, amazed at the effortlessness of her plan and the ease at which it had been executed. Deciding to take no chances, and having seen most horror movies where the discarded body always returned to wreak revenge, Maggie hauled the body through the debris leaving a trail, disturbing the dust.

In his earlier tour Drake had shown Maggie the kitchen, the kitchen with the cellar.

She pulled up the door in the floor and swept the beam down into the darkness.

With all her energy she pushed the slumped body to the edge and over the side.

His fall ended with a dull thud.

Maggie didn't waste time on sentimentality; she slammed down the cellar door and snapped the padlock shut. Drake had used the cellar to store some of his load, hence the new padlock. He had told her that the room beneath the kitchen was small and compact, a litter of discarded furniture and household clutter making exploration of the place too hazardous, but there was enough room just at the base of the steps to store items.

Just enough room for Drake to rest.

Making her way back through the dilapidated farmhouse, Maggie was glad of the evening breeze when finally she emerged from the front of the building. The cooling wind blew over her and stole the beads of sweat which had accumulated over her forehead and into the small of her back. She looked up at the darkening sky with a smile and a sense of satisfaction.

Despite her planning, the years of hatred directed towards both her own family and the family that her sister now belonged to, everything came down to what happened next.

She thought of her mother and father, both dead.

She thought of her sister Natalie and wondered how she felt at the moment; was she scared and afraid, or perhaps she thought her father or the investigator would protect her, keep the monster at bay.

As she thought of the private investigator she couldn't help but let a chuckle escape her lips, wondering if he had given up following her would-be husband around London.

Deciding that it was time to move, time to get the show on the road, Maggie walked across to the outhouses for one last check.

When she was sure that everything was as she needed it to be, she returned to the van, happy in the knowledge that she would soon be heading back to town. She had one quick stop to make, in at the place Drake was staying before heading for the Soderman residence for the beginning of their end.

She reversed the van and edged her way carefully along the track the darkness deepening the further she drove along. At the entrance she waited for a moment, collected herself, leant forward and switched on the radio.

She smiled.

A harbinger of events to come she wondered as the radio was half way through playing The Rolling Stones *Sympathy For The Devil*.

Maggie Dean couldn't help but smile.

Chapter 45

Natalie took her coffee from the vending machine and sat down at the back of the empty restaurant. She took a sip of the dark liquid, wincing at the heat of the drink. She ran her hand through her hair and felt a weariness sweep over her. At the same time she promised herself that it would be her last caffeine intake of the day, at this rate sleep would be a distant visitor for days; despite her tiredness.

Her father was getting dressed and gathering his belongings, hopefully then they would be able to head home. She looked down at her phone and wondered when Harry would be back. She had rung his office and spoken to his assistant who, despite her rather stand-offish tone of voice, had informed her that Harry was in London and would be back later that afternoon. She had offered however, in a much softer voice, to let Harry know that she had rung and that she was fine. Natalie thanked her and hung up, wondering why he hadn't returned her calls. Paranoia began to sink in as it frequently did when it came to the men who had entered and subsequently left her life. Within her close circle of friends back in London, they always teased her about her ability to blow any situation, especially on the subject of men, out of the water. Suddenly Natalie was analyzing every conversation, every meeting that she had had with Harry and every look they had exchanged, since arriving back home. Suddenly questions began reverberating around her mind like one of those silver balls in a pinball machine. *Had she been too full on with him? Had she tried to move too fast or expected too much? Perhaps she should cool things, cancel this evening and spend the evening with her father? Maybe she should let things be and see what happens? For Christ's sake she didn't even live locally anymore and long distance relationships were notoriously bad in the longevity stakes.* At that moment she heard her mother's voice in her mind, *Nat, whatever will be will be!* She smiled at the memory with a mixture of happiness and sadness.

Her phone rang the sound loud against the quietness of the restaurant. She looked down at the number, recognised it and answered the call immediately.

Chapter 46

Harry hated London travel at the best of times, but especially during rush hour. It was a time when most people reverted quickly down the evolutionary scale, where scowls replaced the already lacking smiles and where mere grunting and groaning replaced even the most basic of words as people clambered onto their chosen mode of transport. All around everyone appeared to have a set of headphones plugged into their ears that drowned out the woes of city travelling and condensed them all into their own singular cells of private space.

He had been lucky and as he arrived at the bus stop his connection appeared, so he caught the 521 bus that travelled out of Holborn towards its final destination of Waterloo station. During the ten minute journey Harry found himself squashed together with the other fifty or so rush hour commuters who had crammed their way on to an already overcrowded single decker night bus.

He had tried to wrestle his phone from his pocket but gave it up as a futile gesture, there wasn't enough room. As the bus travelled along its route he lamented the fact that he still hadn't been able to get hold of Natalie and that was troubling him.

Shortly before the doors of the bus had opened he had tried contacting the hospital, asking to be put through to George Soderman but as he wasn't immediate family he was given a polite brush off; the call ended shortly afterwards.

The bus had pulled up on the north-east side of the station and

Harry, along with everyone else, moved as one heaving mass and alighted from their short journey, preparing themselves for the next equally uncomfortable stage. He hurried across the zebra crossing narrowly avoiding a cyclist and his scowling look and then up the steps that led in through the Victory Arch entrance.

Despite hurrying to catch his train he still managed to gaze fleetingly at the statues that adorned either side of the entrance, suppressing the smile that for a moment abated the concern for Natalie. He still recalled with happiness the many trips he had taken to the capital in his younger days and how he always became transfixed by the pure elegance of the carved stonework.

As a child he recalled his father bringing both Harry and his sister up to London on the train where they would meet their Aunt, grab a coffee and a quick catch-up before their father would then head off on the hour long trip returning home, their father saying his goodbyes before disappearing through the barrier to the awaiting train. It was an exchange that happened for a few years in a row, a summer holiday away from home and a chance to spend time with the London relatives that they hardly ever got to see.

Harry made a mental note to call his father in the coming days, maybe after this case was closed he would take a day off and go and visit the old man. Take a bottle of nice wine with him or maybe take him out to dinner.

As he entered the glaring light and concourse of Waterloo Station his thoughts returned to the present as he tried to side-step one person and narrowly dodge another in some parody of a weird game show that pitted your wits against other rushing commuters. He grabbed one of the free newspapers from a kiosk and the bored looking vendor who was working his shift. With a quick stop at the row of departure boards he scanned for his train, found it and then hurried through the masses.

On the train, Harry hurried through several coaches before he found himself a seat, thankful that he had found one, seeing the hoard of commuters who were still scurrying for the same train behind him. Immediately he pulled out his phone and checked the display, no more missed calls.

He hastily scrolled through the list of recently used numbers and pressed the dial button against Natalie's number.

As he waited for the call to be connected he wondered if perhaps he would give his friend Detective Inspector Tony Scott a call, maybe it was time to call in a favour or two, maybe it was time to ask for help. Assuming it wasn't too late.

All thoughts of DI Scott and the cavalry dissipated when Natalie answered breathlessly on the third ring.

Chapter 47

Natalie settled her father onto the sofa in the lounge; the fire was lit and kept the cold at bay with its invisible warm fingers that reached out into the room. Natalie had just managed to change into a fresh pair of jeans and a red sweatshirt that had seen better days, when her mobile had burst into life. She retrieved the device from the back pocket of her jeans, glancing quickly at the caller ID and smiled when she recognised the caller; her father saw the faint trace of a blush over his daughter's face and knew who must be calling.

'Harry!' she said, rushing from the living room and into the kitchen away from the prying ears and eyes of her father. 'I've been trying to ring you.' She sat down at the table feeling a huge wave of emotions rush through her as tears pricked at the corner of her eyes.

She laughed at something he said and also at the state she was in.

She wasn't sure why she had allowed or even managed to let this man in particular get under her skin so much, especially given the short space of time they had actually known one another. Yes she had known him years before but not to speak to. Had there been some kind of subconscious attraction back then; it seemed likely given the way she remembered him where she couldn't remember others who had been her friend. Normally she was so taciturn when it came to meeting men but there was something about this one that she liked, who made her laugh, who looked at her in a way that others hadn't or didn't. With Harry she thought it was more than just about sex for him; with Harry it seemed more emotional, the physical coming a close second.

She was aware that he was saying something; spluttering an apology she asked him to repeat what he had said. The more he told her the more her smile turned into a frown and finally into absolute worry.

Absently she looked towards the back door and the key that remained in the lock.

The window was uncovered, the curtains as yet not pulled across. She stared out into the gloom of the evening sky and felt a shiver crawl down her spine.

'What's her plan Harry?' Natalie asked after telling him about Maggie being at the pub they had been drinking in.

'I wish I knew,' he replied, his voice momentarily drowned out by the voice of the train guard and his station announcements. A few moments passed before Harry could be heard again. 'Just make sure all the doors are shut and bolted yeah, don't open the door to anyone until I get to you okay?'

'Okay! But what if...' she let her sentence trail off unfinished.

'Listen to me Natalie, if anything happens, anything, dial 9-9-9 and don't try anything stupid yeah?'

'How long are you going to be?' she asked knowing it wouldn't be quick enough.

'I'll get there as soon as I can and Natalie,'

'Yes?'

'I'm sorry.'

'What have you got to be sorry about?'

'For not doing what I should have been doing, protecting you.'

'Harry...'

'The train's starting to leave, I'll call you when...' his call ended as his signal became lost, swallowed in the void of a tunnel. Natalie stared at the phone for a few moments wondering if he would ring back. When he didn't she slid the phone back into the rear pocket of her jeans. She sat there wondering when everything had become such a mess, when it was that everything had descended into some parody of an ITV drama. She felt the biting cold of dread seep through her thin red sweater. For a moment she became lost in thought, brought alarmingly back to reality by the sound of the doorbell ringing. Her breath caught in her throat as time, for that moment, appeared to stop. Seconds later she heard her father's voice.

'I'll get it, it's probably Harry,' he yelled, quickly followed by the sound of his footsteps as he reached the front door and turned the lock.

'DAD!' she shouted, surprised to find her voice working and the fear that emanated with it.

But it was too late.

Chapter 48

'Damn it!' Harry cursed, and for the second time that day incurred the look and unspoken wrath of those around him. This time an older lady who had sat down next to him only moments ago. He heard her tut her final disapproval before looking around the carriage, no doubt searching for another seat away from the degenerate she had unwittingly sat down next to who had not only been using his mobile phone in a designated quiet zone but who spouted obscenities when it wouldn't work. Harry noted the resigned sigh as she failed to find another seat and instead watched her reflection in the window as she unfolded the newspaper from her bag, no doubt saving the details so that she could regurgitate them later with her high profile husband or with the ladies dining circle.

Harry slumped in his seat, unable to get comfortable, finally choosing to lean his head against the coolness of the glass.

Damn phone! He silently cursed, annoyed that he hadn't checked his battery on his phone, and irritated more than anything because now he had no way of keeping in contact with Natalie until he arrived back home.

Closing his eyes against the incessant bass emanating from the seat in front of him and trying to banish the insufferable contemplation of the journey ahead, he tried to think things through in his mind, tried to work out what he was going to do and more importantly, if he had time in which to do it.

The train rumbled on as spatters of rain began to plaster the windows.

His eyes were tired and coupled with the gentle rhythmic vibration of the train moving over the tracks it wasn't long before his eyes were closing as he became lost in sleep.

It was not a peaceful sleep. His dreams were littered with faces and memories that mingled with one another and became an anthology of worrying scenes played out in private viewing for the man who lolled against the window, occasionally making him groan in his sleep and giving the lady next to him more ammunition for her soon to be told tale.

When Maggie Dean's face appeared in front of his eyes, snarling with a grin of pure malevolence, he awoke with a start. The lady next to him gave another sigh and returned to her newspaper.

Harry wiped his eyes in an effort to push the haze of sleep aside.

The train was just pulling into Grateley. Harry looked around the carriage and saw that it had emptied somewhat. Looking out of the window he noticed that those who stood on the platform waiting to board were drenched.

Great! He thought, wishing that he had brought his overcoat with him.

Pulling his mobile out of his pocket he tried the power button but despite a brief show of the service provider's logo the phone died.

The sound of the guard blowing his whistle was shortly followed by the slow movement of the train departing the station. Harry's thoughts immediately returned to Natalie and her sister and what the hell he was going to do.

Chapter 49

Natalie stood frozen to the spot, unable to move, her limbs solid and stone-like. Standing in the entrance way to the house stood her sister. Gone was the dark hair, no doubt a wig, her hair now blonde and pulled back into a ponytail. Her features were pale and sullen, her eyes dark voids of emptiness that sent waves of unease through Natalie. Her father stood close by in a state of shock, unsure of what to do, what to say; he was immobile.

Natalie looked at her sister and felt that familiar chill of apprehension rush through her. It was all her bogeymen from her childhood appearing at once, it was Freddie Kruger and Michael Myers, it was all the monsters from childhood cartoons, except this one was unpleasantly real.

What was more frightening was the fact that they looked so similar so much so that they could have been twins. It was not a pleasant feeling and it sent a fresh wave of coldness through her already chilled body.

'Well isn't this cosy?' she said, her voice calm and collected, as if this was an everyday occurrence.

'What do you want?' George stammered, much to the chagrin of Maggie Dean.

'Oh come on George; let's not play dumb, it's far too late for that.' George Soderman went to make a move but the girl in the entrance way was much quicker. The gleaming coldness of the gun barrel was upon him before he could catch his breath.

'Dad!' Natalie called.

Maggie Dean entered the house, her eyes moving coldly between father and daughter, with a satisfied smile etched over her face. In a fluid movement Maggie pulled a bag from behind her and slid it across the hallway floor to land at Natalie's feet.

'Open it! Take out the cuffs and come over here, slowly.' Natalie did as ordered, tears pricking at the corners of her eyes, as she fought to control her emotions, not wanting to appear weak. 'Good! Give the cuffs to George sis, then put your hands behind your back like the good girl I know you are.'

'You know shit about me.' Natalie said, surprised at the venom that came with the words she spoke. She instantly regretted her anger, not wanting her unstable sister to lash out.

'Well, well, my little sister does have bite to her, good to know.' George Soderman looked at his daughter with a lost smile and eyes that gave away his look of failure, of disappointment with himself. It had been his job to protect his daughter no matter what, he had tried, but ultimately he had failed.

Natalie turned and placed her hands behind her back.

The snap of the cuffs echoed around the hallway as Natalie felt an inane urge to laugh out loud at the ridiculousness of what was happening. From the lounge came the low sound of Billie Holiday singing *Crazy He Calls Me*. Biting down on her lip, Natalie closed her eyes, her mind racing, trying to think what to do next.

Harry was on his way out of London but she wasn't sure what time he would get here; by then God only knew what would have happened. She thought about her mobile in her back pocket, thankful that her ring tone was not one of those loud and prolonged tunes, but she also wished that her tone had been set to silent.

If only she could get a message to him.

Maggie bent down and took a second pair of cuffs from the bag and snapped then hastily around George Soderman's awaiting hands.

'Follow me and don't make a sound, either of you, and trust me when I say I am more than happy to use this,' she said, her eyes lowering to the handgun.

Father and daughter fell silent as they were led out of the front door and towards a waiting white van. The doors were open and ready, the black mouth of the interior like the yawning entrance of a gigantic vast cave ready to swallow them whole.

Natalie managed to get herself up and into the van; stumbling in the darkness she fell against the wheel arch with a thud. She felt her phone in her pocket slide from her pocket and rattle to the floor.

Cursing, Natalie tried to right herself and move her hands from the rear but found nothing.

'Hey hey George what's this?' Their captor said, reaching into his back pocket and relieving him of his phone. 'Don't think you're going to need that anymore.' Maggie clasped the phone and shoved the man head first into the rear of the van, watching with enjoyment as he scurried like a rat into the darkness.

Joining her captives in the back Maggie crouched down in front of Natalie.

'Best check you hey sis?' she said, seemingly more relaxed at present. She turned her sister and searched her front pockets before patting down her rear pockets, although somewhat lackadaisical in her approach. Happy that no phone could be found and wanting to be on her way, Maggie jumped down from the van and slammed the doors shut.

Realising that the entrance to the house was still open and that that alone might invite inquisitive neighbours, she made her way to the front door, pausing at the entrance. She still had Soderman's phone in her hand which she discarded, throwing it onto the hallway floor.

Shutting the door for the last time, Maggie Dean felt her body tighten with anticipation of what was to come.

With a smile she returned to the van and climbed into the driver's seat, turned the ignition key and edged carefully out of the drive.

The road was clear and a quick glance at the houses she drove past revealed windows of darkness and empty driveways, something she was glad of.

At the end of Hayward Way she turned and then a few moments later turned left again, this time onto Bridge Road. She drove slowly over the bridge and past the entrance to the hotel she had stayed at.

Finally she was out of the village, all without encountering any other vehicles. Despite her bravado, Maggie found her stomach doing somersaults with nervous excitement.

The moment she had been planning for was near to being realised.

She leant forward and switched on the radio, some song covered with a dance beat over the top was part way through, but Maggie was in too good a mood to let the irritation of a good song covered badly ruin her day.

In the back of the van Natalie and George Soderman sat close to one another but both were symbolically miles apart. They sat in silence, each lost within their own dark thoughts. Unease and apprehension were very close and very unwelcome visitors.

Chapter 50

Harry was hot, his shirt drenched in sweat. The train had been a few minutes later arriving at his destination than planned, delayed by a mixture of engineering works and signal failures. Fighting his way from the train, along with the mass of nightly commuters, he rushed through the ticket barriers, ignoring glances by the cantankerous and the irritated as he barged through. His concerns lay elsewhere and far outstripped any sense of guilt for his rudeness.

Outside the train station the cool night air was welcome against his face as he rushed out onto the pavement towards his office and to his car. Just as the train had been due to arrive he had fired up his mobile but despite a brief flirtation with powering up, the mobile had died.

The lights were still on in both his and the solicitor's office above. With a brief glance through the door he saw the cleaner busy at work.

He waved quickly, wondering if he should pop into his office to see if any messages had been left. Deciding against it Harry climbed into his car and reversed quickly out of the car park, all the while hoping and praying that Natalie and George Soderman were at home, safe from harm.

His hope died a quick and agonizing death when he saw the lights on and then found the front door unlocked and George Soderman's mobile discarded on the floor.

'Shit!' he said, giving up his search, realising it was too late, after shouting out both their names and receiving nothing but silence in return.

He picked up Soderman's mobile and scrolled through to Natalie's number and quickly rang it, hoping that they had gone for a drink or a mid-evening walk. He knew he was clutching at straws but he grasped them with hope and held on with both hands as though for dear life.

Her mobile rang and rang, eventually her voicemail cut in.

Harry entered the lounge which was missing its main ingredient, people. The fire was lit, the heat warm and welcoming. Music played low from the stereo, the song was old and bluesy, something he didn't recognise. All that was missing was George Soderman sitting by the fire with his crossword and glass of wine with perhaps Natalie sitting opposite lost in a magazine or a book.

Harry sat himself down upon the sofa, fighting the effect the heat was having on him. If he closed his eyes he felt sure he would sleep for a week despite the situation he found himself in.

He looked down at George's mobile in his hand, gazed at the signal bar as it changed between 3G and GPRS, a signal that fluctuated between poor and good.

Then it hit him.

Natalie's mobile had not gone straight to voicemail; therefore it was on, somewhere. And if the mobile phone was on, it was traceable.

The thought banished his fatigue and renewed his energy with vigour.

He had the software on his computer at work, if he went back now perhaps he could…a ray of hope suddenly began to grow inside of him, it was small but it was something.

Taking Soderman's mobile with him he paused in the hallway and took the keys that were left on the side. He turned off the hall lights and locked the door, ever secure.

He thought again about ringing his contact on the force, DI Scott, but by the time he got through and relayed the story it may be too late.

Harry started the engine, switched off the radio, not in the mood for any music. He needed to think, and he needed to think fast.

Time was against him, as was the traffic.

He hit every red light between Redburn and the city which did nothing to help his mood.

When finally he arrived at work, parking haphazardly as he rushed into the office he logged his computer on and loaded the *Cell Trace* mobile phone tracking software. He signed in and entered the details then clicked on the trace button. Harry watched the screen nervously. He sat in his office, the only light the flicker of his monitor. Shadows danced all around him but he neither cared nor did anything to dispel the gloom; his eyes remained fixated on the screen.

Finally the map appeared.

Beep!

A small yellow icon appeared on the map, flicking on and off, on and off. The tracing software would update every fifteen seconds to update the location but that would be of no use to him. The tracing system was new, had only been setup within the last few weeks and in that time Harry had yet to set up the system to access it from his own mobile device. He cursed his laziness, if that's what it had been, under his breath.

He looked back at the screen, the location had updated but the target was not moving very fast, that was the only saving grace. But that could be a red herring, with the phone moving there was always a chance of losing the signal.

But what concerned him the most was the location in which the trace was going.

He printed the map, locked the screen and left the office.

Outside the rain that had been threatening to pour down was now venting its anger with full force. Harry ran the short distance from his office to his car, ignoring the wetness that streaked his body and the worry that was snapping at his heels.

He had a trace on Natalie's mobile phone and time was an unknown luxury he didn't have; the last thing he wanted was to have the trail go cold.

He just prayed that he wasn't too late already.

Chapter 51

In the back of the van driven by Maggie Dean, George Soderman was thankful for one thing, and that was the sanctuary that the darkness offered. Within the silent stillness he was thankful that Natalie couldn't see him crying. Tears streamed down his face and stung his skin. He shuddered, his hands gripping one another in tight balls, trying to do his best to keep his feelings hidden from his daughter.

Natalie hadn't uttered a word since the van door had been closed.

In those last dying seconds before the door had blocked what little light had emitted from the driveway lights both his daughter and he had exchanged a look. It was a look that spoke a thousand words.

They were in trouble.

They had no idea where they were being taken.

No one, as yet, knew that they were missing.

The van began to slow, turned off the road onto an uneven surface that bumped and shook the van and those inside.

Natalie grunted as she was tossed from one side of the van to the other, colliding with her father.

He helped her as best he could but when he heard the sound of her tears breaking through the darkness the sound made his heart lurch.

As a father, and as a man, he had never before felt so useless, so powerless.

Over the years he had been there to help pick up the pieces when boyfriends came and went, when her mother had passed away. He had been there when she was just down, when she was sick and needed looking after. All those times when he threw his arms around her, held her close, taken her into his arms and told her that everything was going to be alright.

But now?

Now those words, those actions, seemed redundant and superfluous as well as near impossible.

The van came to a halt.

Inadvertently both Natalie and her father held their breath.

They heard their captor get out of the van but the door to their incarcerated surroundings did not open. In the dark they stared towards the door intently, frightened, anxious and pensive.

A grating noise came from outside but was gone as quickly as it came.

Moments later Maggie Dean returned to the van, slamming the door shut.

The van moved forward, slowly, carefully, as though the terrain was tricky to drive upon.

Once more the van came to a halt.

The driver climbed down from her seat and disappeared into silence. No sound of approach. Only the uncomfortable uncertainty of what was to come.

George Soderman and his daughter waited in silence. For a brief moment Soderman wondered if this was what it felt like before you were executed. When the hood was placed over your head, your world turning black, when the breath of your executioner was so close it was cloying.

Outside the van they heard footsteps crunching over the ground.

Then a pause, when nothing made a sound or moved, silence both lord and master.

Seconds later the van doors opened.

Chapter 52

Harry drove blind.

He had no idea what he was heading into, if she would still be there or indeed if the owner of the mobile and the device were even together.

When finally he had cleared the succession of red lights that did their best to slow his progress he made it to the back roads and put his foot harder against the accelerator. He was on the outskirts of town now, in the middle of countryside littered with farm houses, dairy and self access storage units.

The rain had ceased for the moment, offering Harry at least a chance of getting closer to his target. As he approached the last known location he pulled into a lay-by, switched on his interior light and checked the location on the printed page against his road map.

He was in the right place but that was it.

Outside the sky was dark offering no pinpoints of light that represented houses or any other buildings that were occupied. He bit down on his lip with a combination of trepidation and fear whilst he felt his stomach lurch.

What if this was it.

What if this was where the trail went dead, as well as…

Harry stopped himself from finishing the sentence; he let it disappear into the dark void of night which enveloped him.

Shutting off the interior light he pushed open the car door and climbed out. He stood on the road side and gazed around him.

He had driven these roads a hundred times, maybe more, but he did not recall any type of building out this way that would give Maggie Dean the isolation she so obviously needed for her two hostages.

He thought about calling in help again, but the time factor mooted the idea.

He was on his own.

He would have to find Natalie and her father under his own steam.

Annoyed with himself for being ushered out of the way like some novice, wet behind the ears, trainee investigator, he swore aloud and returned to the car. He couldn't believe he had been played like he had. He couldn't believe that Maggie Dean had been as close as she had. Harry thought back to yesterday when he had met Natalie for a drink; God was that only yesterday, he thought scornfully. The woman with the dark hair sitting at the bar, the same woman he had said hello to. Maggie Dean, so close all the bloody time. So close and probably laughing at them, at him, always with her plan set out in front of her. A road map for her vendetta.

He grunted, closed his eyes to block the rage that was beginning to build and slammed his hands against the steering wheel. He had been so damn stupid, utterly brainless and dim-witted.

Pulling the car out of the lay-by in a trail of spinning gravel and squealing tyres, Harry decided to travel this stretch of road for a while longer. He would give it a few minutes. After that he would have to head back, admit defeat, call in the big guns and pray to God that it wasn't too late.

His mind was consumed with anger whilst his insides felt as though he was riding a rollercoaster at the fair. His eyes were so distracted by his absolute need to find Maggie Dean's bolt-hole that he missed the barely concealed turning on the left, and a place that in the deep recesses of his mind, he knew about.

The old farm buildings had been owned by the Thomas family for three generations prior to a greedy heir wasting money and desecrating the family business.

Harry drove on.

Chapter 53

'Both of you, out now!' Maggie Dean said, standing in the open doorway, both father and daughter looking like the scared and frightened creatures they were. George Soderman came first, doing his best to offer any kind of bravado, trying to keep face in the uncertainty that was their immediate future. He jumped down to the gravel track, stumbled and found himself almost kneeling at his captor's side. The irony wasn't lost on Maggie Dean who smiled before returning her attention to her sister.

The old man would be of no trouble, that much was evident; he was too old and weak with fear. But the girl, her sister, she had guts, Maggie could tell that now and that posed an issue for her, a pleasing one though.

Natalie Soderman paused on the edge of the van's rear doors, looking at her surroundings as though she was spending a night out at camp and not thinking of a way to escape. Maggie leant forward and pulled the woman's arm, almost dragging her from the rear of the van.

As Natalie's feet hit the ground she turned her ankle and began falling. She turned, unsure of where her fall would take her. With her legs buckling as her feet sank into a puddle, Natalie saw her only means of safety. Reaching out with her hands Natalie gripped the fence post that stood at an angle as though it was ready to topple over. Barbed wire that had seen better days looked menacing and threatening, blocking her way.

As she turned to face her father and her captor she snagged a section of her sweatshirt on the wire fence. Pulling away the material came free, lodging itself on the wire spike.

Losing patience, Maggie ushered both her captives away from the van and towards the outbuildings without giving the van a second look. She wanted them both locked up and out of sight; she didn't trust the shadows that enveloped her. She had started to have an extreme dislike of the sound the trees made as they swayed unassumingly all around her. It sounded like an orchestra containing hundreds of whispering voices, all chattering incoherently.

In one hand she held her torch, lighting the way for Soderman to follow with Natalie close behind. Before opening the rear doors she had unlocked the entrance to the outbuilding, the same door they now walked through.

Maggie laughed as both wrinkled their noses at the smell, or maybe it was the surroundings, or maybe it was the realisation that this was the place where they would end their days.

The captive pair remained close to one another, their eyes wide and frightened, looking like two children who had wandered out into the darkness late at night.

'Well isn't this nice?' Maggie said, shining the torch from father to daughter and back again. She ran the beam the entire length of her sister's body, revelling in the obvious discomfort both the attention and the light was having on her. She moved in close, so close that her breath prickled the skin of her sister, goose bumps dancing over her skin along with a shudder of fear.

Maggie laughed.

Leaning forward she planted a kiss on her sister's cheek.

'Been waiting for this moment for a long, long time sis.' Her voice was calm and fully charged with foreboding menace.

'What do you want?' Natalie stammered, trying to hold herself together but on the brink of losing it.

'All in good time, all in good time.'

Maggie moved the torch beam and shone it over George Soderman. He closed his eyes and turned his face away from the light, the beam stinging his vision. She could see his rage; it was bubbling beneath the surface like a predator waiting to strike.

She smiled.

It was good to see their reserve, their cool aloofness near to braking point.

'What....' Natalie began to say, her voice rising with anger with each letter spoken, but Maggie cut her words to silence with a sharp turn. She pointed the torch directly into her eyes.

'I said all in good time.' Her words were delivered coldly with an icy stare to match. Maggie Dean let the gaze linger and the silence grow.

Behind her Soderman moved, agitated, no doubt frustrated that he could do little to help; it was as she wanted it. The dynamic was set; it would be to her advantage to play with it.

'Right then, best we get started.' Maggie was quick on her feet. She lowered the beam and crossed the short distance to Soderman. She grabbed him by the cuffs and led him from the building.

Natalie shouted and moved as if to follow.

'No, no, no... you stay right where you are sis.' Maggie had the gun in her hand; she had pulled it from the waistband of her clothing. She nestled the barrel end of the gun into the side of the old man, enjoying his discomfort and her sister's horror. 'I haven't even started with you yet.' With that she guided the man from the building, slammed the door shut and snapped the lock into place.

She heard Natalie reach the door; seconds later came the thud, followed by another thud as she took out her frustration on the door.

Maggie returned to the door, laughed at the constant clamour from within.

'Make all the noise you like, there is no one around here for miles.'

Maggie Dean hauled George Soderman across the driveway, their footsteps crunching on the gravel and echoing into the night sky. His protesting words of gallantry fell on deaf ears as captor led captive into the shadowy ruin that had once been the farmhouse.

The torchlight did little to dispel the gloom, whilst the doorway groaned its displeasure at the late night visitors and the stone flooring echoed their footsteps.

She led him through to the kitchen, pushing him down into one of the remaining unbroken kitchen chairs. Maggie busied herself, she left the kitchen and Soderman could hear her dragging through a heavy object that scraped over the floor with a harsh grating sound.

Blinded by the dark and with no other obvious means of escape, George could only wait until the circle of light identified her location. He waited in the chair, the cold circling like hungry vultures around his chest. He was wheezing; the slight rattle on his chest when he exhaled told him all he needed to know.

He thought of Natalie; he could barely hear her rage as she continued to kick out at a door that would not give and would not budge.

He thought of Harry, wondered where he was.

For a few seconds he felt a hint of anger directed at the man he had charged with protecting his daughter. He knew they liked one another, that was all too evident to see and as a father he wanted nothing more than for his daughter to settle down with someone he knew would look after her, but the investigator had slipped up and he had slipped up in a major way.

The devil had been at the door and he had let him in.

His nemesis appeared in the kitchen, the light displaying a hatch in the floor, a cellar.

He gulped with fear, his Adam's apple feeling suddenly too large for his throat.

She walked over to the hatch, bent down and took a key from her pocket. She unlocked the padlock and drew up the hatch door with what passed as relative caution for a woman who had kidnapped two people and killed another two.

'Guess where you're going George?' she said, not turning to meet his eyes. She shone her torch down into the depths of the hole, crouched down and, for a few seconds, she seemed intrigued by something, her gaze engaged, her captive momentarily forgotten.

George thought about what he was going to do, but not for long.

It was now or never.

With everything he could muster he sprang to his feet as fast as he could and headed in the direction from which he had been brought in.

Maggie spun on her heels, surprised by the older man's sudden flight.

She followed quickly, hunter gathering her prey.

She was on him quickly, slamming down the butt of the gun over the back of his head and watching with satisfaction as he fell to the floor with a crash, collapsing in a heap.

'What did you think you were doing George?' she asked, her voice once again sounding calm and cool. She aimed the gun at him and fired.

His protestations ended as quickly as they had begun.

Outside, the kicking of the outhouse door ceased instantly.

'Won't be doing that again will you George?'

She dragged the body through to the kitchen and to the edge of the hatch. Pushing with all her strength she tipped the body of George Soderman over the edge of the cellar entrance and watched his body disappear into the gloom.

'George, meet Drake, Drake meet George, I hope you'll both be eternally happy together.'

She slammed the hatch down and clicked the lock into place.

Returning to the item she had hauled in earlier she opened the lid and began pouring the contents all around the room, the stench beginning to burn her nostrils.

Outside she heard Natalie shouting George's name, becoming more and more frantic with each call. Maggie Dean couldn't help but smile.

Now was the time she had been looking forward to.

She dropped the can of petrol and made her way back outside.

Chapter 54

Harry pulled the car to a stop just short of the gravel track that was almost hidden from sight. He switched the headlights off and sat for a moment in the car, his heart racing and his body sweating despite the cold.

It was amazing what data the brain collected and held without you knowing about it. Harry had driven on for another mile or so before his brain had replayed the image of the road near to the lay-by he had rested in, along with the hidden road entrance had been a brief biography of the place. It was perfect; he berated himself for not thinking of it sooner.

He looked at the break in the bushes, the beginnings of what was a near perfectly concealed dirt track. He had reversed quickly and made his way back along the dark and deserted road on a hunch, a gut feeling that told him it was worth checking; what else had he to go on?

Pushing open his door he stepped out into the night, the bitterness in the air wrapping its icy and unfriendly tendrils around him, squeezing him, as if warning him to go back, to keep away.

He recovered a small bag from the boot.

The bag contained a few items he never travelled without.

He took his torch and tested the beam, its light was strong, a good solid white shaft of light. The bag contained first aid, a blanket and a bottle of water. He hoped he would have use for them. Setting off along the track he tried to walk on the edges, avoiding the gravel, the crunch of his feet against ground echoing loudly around him, announcing his arrival.

The lane was pitch-black, inky in its denseness. The sky above seemed hidden, as though the trees were leaning over with their branch-like arms acting as a shield.

The beam found a gate. With the bag over his shoulder he pocketed the torch for a moment and moved around the gate, not wanting to risk opening it for fear of tripping an alarm or making a sound. He took it carefully, not wanting to snag his footing.

Harry paused.

Listened.

All he heard was the whispering of the woods. It was something that did little to scare him; he had grown up living opposite dense thick woodland on a road local inhabitants had wonderfully nicknamed Ghost Lane. Countless times he had been out in the dead of night wandering in the darkness, listening to the woods talking and the night creatures scurrying; it was almost a sense of comfort and not the opposite.

He shone his torch over the ground and found impressions of tyre tracks.

As he moved further onto the property Harry located a white van, and the old Thomas farmhouse.

His body involuntarily shuddered. He wasn't sure if the shudder has been caused by the cold chilly air or the worry of what he would find at the farmhouse.

Carefully he made his way along the track.

Chapter 55

'Where's my father?' Natalie asked, her voice surprisingly calm despite the obvious rage that bubbled inside of her coupled with concern for the situation she now found herself in. She thought about her father and about Harry.

'Dead!' her sister replied with a tone of satisfaction and almost glee. 'Well, actually your real father, our father, is dead whilst George is slightly injured, incapacitated shall we say but it amounts to the same thing.' Again that same smile of intense fulfilment, and that same gleeful, darkly marauding grin.

Natalie's expression didn't change; her eyes were directed towards her sister, unblinking and for the first time Maggie would go so far as to say unreadable, almost. She was slightly in awe of her sister, for a few brief moments. In all the pictures she had seen of her back at the house she thought she would be a spineless, daddy's girl, the kind of girl who would drop her bottom lip and await the help of a rugged boyfriend or overly protective father. Instead Natalie spoke with the kind of calmness that worried her, albeit in a curious sense.

'Why?' her sister said, voice low and hushed, almost too weak in volume to hear, despite the closeness of their bodies in the relative gloom of the outhouse.

'Oh come on now sis, is it really too hard to figure out?'

Natalie said nothing, her thoughts consumed by the notion of her foster father lying injured some place close by whilst she played guessing games with her estranged sister in a dark and dank cell.

Maggie looked over her shoulder as if someone had walked behind her.

She looked back at her captive, her face, for a brief moment, etched with concern, some of the smugness depleted but it returned quick enough.

'I haven't finished with you yet,' she said, stepping over to the door, listening for something that had not yet reached Natalie's ears. Natalie saw her sister reach into the waistband of her trousers and pull the gun from beneath.

Something had spooked her.

Chapter 56

Harry gazed at the open rear doors of the white van, his eyes taking in the vast darkness of within as if expecting something awful and vile to emerge from its sinister depths. A quick search using his torch had found no sign of captives except for Natalie's mobile that lay as if dropped in the far corner near to the driver's cab.

He grabbed the phone, scrolled through the menu system until he found the option to silence the ring tone, then he placed it in his pocket, sub-consciously willing the moment when he could hand it back over to her, alive and well.

Clambering from the back of van he peered around the side and gazed at his surroundings, saw the barbed wire fence and… As he moved closer he shone the beam of his torch over the wire fence and found a small patch of red material. The red material fluttered in the gentle breeze, a lone piece of blood red colour against the drabness of its surroundings.

Turning around he took a look at the remote structure set against a backdrop of an ever darkening sky. Even from this vantage point he could see the state of the farmhouse. He crept around, trying to make as little noise as possible. He glanced to his left and saw the silhouette of the outbuildings, perhaps once they housed the livestock and suppliers, now they were simply left to fall into ruin.

Something caught his eye over to his left, a glint of something unknown.

He retreated around the back of the van and began to make his way towards the first of the outbuildings. All around him the trees whispered incessantly as though chattering amongst themselves in a foreign tongue, the investigator not privy to their hushed words.

At the end of the first stone building he waited. He lowered his bag from his shoulder and pushed it against the building, the item was instantly swallowed by the gloominess.

He felt ridiculously like a character from a Wild West film as though coming into the ghost town to face an unknown nemesis who was watching him from one of the shady windows.

Harry caught his breath and listened for any sound out of the ordinary.

Aside from the whispering of the trees everything else was still and quiet.

He moved around the corner of the first stone building, his feet crunching down over dried twigs and broken glass that seemed to echo around the yard area.

He stopped dead, not wanting to move another foot in front of the other.

He wondered if he had given himself away, if Maggie had heard his approach. If she had heard or seen him, then she was being coy about coming out to confront the investigator.

He waited for a moment, convinced that he had heard voices nearby. Ahead of him he saw the row of outbuildings. He studied them quickly, the first building looked to have had a new door fitted, whilst the other buildings had doors that were in varying states of disrepair, some doors were hanging from broken hinges, panels were missing and what was left creaked with a groan in the light breeze.

He swung his torch beam towards the first door and caught sight of a gleaming padlock that was unclasped and hanging on the closed door.

Harry looked across at the farmhouse and wondered again if someone was watching him from one of the windows. It was as he looked more intently at the front of the dilapidated building that he caught the faint odour on the breeze.

It was unmistakably petrol, and not just a little drop.

Harry tensed.

He looked from outbuilding to farmhouse, torn between the two.

He didn't like the quietness. Natalie and George had to be here someplace.

Moving from the side of the building, Harry made his way quickly across the short expanse of gravel and made for the front of the farmhouse.

The smell of spilt petrol and damp mingled to make an uninviting stench.

Focusing the light of the torch through the doorway, the beam did its best to break the inky barrier in front, but the dark was so dense that it managed only a short distance.

Deciding that he had only one option left open to him, Harry entered the farmhouse.

Chapter 57

Natalie had shifted on the discarded crate she was using as a seat, her mouth ready to scream when Maggie had turned the gun to point straight at her. Whatever Natalie had wanted to scream had disappeared in the instant the gun had been pointed in her direction. The cold grey barrel that gazed at her with its menacing coin sized cavity silenced her scream, stole her fight and crumbled some of her tenacity, albeit temporarily.

Had she really heard a sound, was it possible that she had heard a noise from outside through the thickness of the stone clad walls? Maggie kept the gun trained on her prey whilst she turned her head and looked towards the doorway.

Nothing made a sound, no footsteps approached but she was sure she had heard something.

Walking on nimble silent feet she reached the door and pushed it open ever so slightly.

The sky was that strange mixture of colouring at dusk, as daylight had almost given in to the darkness. The sky was clear, the trees and farmhouse dark shapes against the backdrop of the evening sky.

Maggie looked hard but saw no signs of movement and heard nothing other than the whispering trees and the nocturnal creatures who spoke out against the silence.

She closed the door and walked over to where her sister sat, arms behind her cuffed, her eyes wide with a mixture of both fear and anger.

'You did well didn't you?' Maggie said, pulling over another discarded crate and sitting herself opposite her sister, the gun resting over her lap, her right hand enclosed around the butt of the weapon.

Natalie said nothing, just looked at her sister with eyes that looked to have lost the fight. It was something that both fascinated and amused Maggie in equal measure. It was the same look that she herself had grown up with, the look was a constant reminder of her introduction to a world that was, for her, full of setbacks and knocks, trials and tribulations and no hero to save her.

'As a little girl I loved reading the Famous Five stories, read them over and over again, some of the books were nearly falling apart by the time I had finished with them. And do you know why I loved reading them so much?' Maggie didn't give her sister much of a chance to consider, let alone reply to her question before launching into her own response.

'I loved those books because it was how I wanted to live, how I wanted it to be. I wanted to be a part of something, a group, a gang, but no one wanted to know me. They always called me a loner, made me out to be some kind of oddball.

Of course Dad didn't help, he truly was an oddball, but then I guess you wouldn't remember that, you weren't around then.' Natalie listened, suddenly attentive, spellbound by the tale her sister was telling. She was finally getting the answer to the question she had kept asking in her mind. *Why did Maggie want to harm her, what had she done to her?* The simple answer, Natalie thought, was actually nothing. It was more a case of harm by association. She listened some more, realising that her sister had resorted to speaking in a softer, calmer, quieter tone of voice.

'Then again mother and I didn't realise what Dad was up to half of the time, I guess we should have guessed. Mother should have known from the first time he hit her and locked her under the stairs for two days. Rumours circulated but nothing happened. No police visits. Just word of mouth from the local oddball, every community has one.' Maggie laughed, looked up and stared directly into the eyes of her sister but she wasn't really looking at her sister, she was seeing through the looking glass, a gateway into her past, seeing a window of time that had long since past.

'Have you ever read the Famous Five?' Maggie Dean asked, her voice sounding lost, childlike almost. Natalie nodded her head, saying that she had. She didn't mention that they were the first books that her foster father had given her. They had been his own, he had collected them when he was younger, had enjoyed reading them. Countless nights he had sat with Natalie reading from the opening of *Five on Treasure Island*, to the closing pages of *Five Are Together Again*. A smile spread across Natalie's face but quickly vanished when she thought of George.

'So you know what I am talking about, I can imagine you as Anne, and me as George.' Again Maggie laughed, but it was a cold and unfriendly laugh as she recalled something dark. 'I remember mother had bought me a couple of those books from a charity shop, they were my pride and joy. Do you know what Dad did with them? He burnt them in one of his drunken rages. Burnt them right in front of my eyes, before giving me a hiding because I was showing an interest in something.'

'God!' Natalie said, not realising that she had said anything at all.

'My point is, you were lucky. You were given a way out. I wasn't. I had to suffer in silence, no one came to help me, and then when I started developing, that's when dad really started taking an interest in me, do you know how it feels to be in bed, shaking with fear as someone stands over you, drunken breath pouring over you as his wandering hands came beneath the cover?'

Natalie shuddered, shook her head but said nothing, she didn't dare saying anything, she couldn't trust her voice.

Maggie stood up, her voice rising in tone and temper. Her body was agitated, almost erratic. She waved the gun from side to side, laughed at unspoken jokes and locked eyes with her sister, but said nothing.

'How can you blame me?' Natalie finally said, her voice quiet, demure, measured almost.

'Because you got the life I should have had.' Maggie finally said. 'Because I tried to end it all, I tried to get out, to take my mother out too.' Her words were louder now, her strides around the building longer. 'I was the one who called the police, I shopped my own father and what good did it do me, answer me that?'

Silence fell between them as Maggie Dean marched towards her sister, her eyes dark and full of rage and raised the gun towards her sister.

Chapter 58

The overwhelming smell of petrol had engulfed his nostrils and clogged his throat like thick smoke. Harry moved from one room to the other, sidestepping fallen debris whilst watching his step for the silent forms that lay hidden in the darkness waiting for the torchlight to pick them out; a broken chair and a discarded box doing their best to bring him crashing to the ground.

He paused at the base of the stairs; saw the disrepair; steps missing whilst others looked unstable and not fit for walking on. Giving the stairs a miss for the moment, the investigator carried on his search of the ground floor and entered the kitchen.

As he flashed the beam around the room he noticed the layers of dust that covered the worktops and the discarded leftovers of mugs, plates and long since unusable pots and pans.

But it was as he lowered the beam over the floor that he noticed the trapdoor in the floor. What was more concerning was the fresh foot prints close by and what looked like drag marks, freshly made with footprints that were not his own. Here dust had been disturbed and recently. His heart jumped as he noted the gleaming padlock that secured the door. It was new, without a doubt added recently.

He moved closer to the trap door, crouched down and tested the lock.

It was then that the thudding began.

His heart stammered as he rocked on his heels, nearly falling backwards. Recovering his position he leant in closer to the door, tried the padlock in a futile dream of finding it unclasped. It was not. The lock was clicked shut and further more it was solid.

'Hello?' Harry called out tentatively.

No response.

He waited a second or two before calling out again.

'Hello?'

'Harry!' came the faint voice, unmistakably belonging to George Soderman.

'Christ! George, are you hurt?' Harry asked, his voice coming in quick gasps as he nervously looked around, half expecting Maggie Dean to emerge out of the shadows.

She didn't.

But that didn't stop the hairs rising at the base of Harry's neck or the ice cold fear rush through his veins.

'Are you hurt?' Harry repeated, flashing the torch around the floor in the vain attempt at hoping the key would be someplace handy. A smile creased his lips. Maggie Dean was not that sloppy. All of this had been planned and executed well.

'I'm okay Harry…'

'Natalie?' Harry cut in. 'Is she with you?'

'I think she is still in one of the outbuildings but that was a while ago.'

'Okay George, I'll be back for you.'

'Harry?'

'Yes?'

'Just get to my daughter in time that is all I ask.'

'Okay.'

Harry turned quickly on his heels and swept the room with his torch, searching the kitchen for any available weapon but finding none.

Deciding that he had little time to play with, Harry left the kitchen and made his way through the dilapidated building and out into the cool evening air.

Ahead of him he saw the outbuildings and began heading towards them.

Gravel crunched beneath his feet but he had little to no choice; there was no other way of approaching the buildings silently.

He raised the torch and checked the first building, the padlock was open. He swept the beam to the second building but found the door hanging half off, no padlock was going to secure that door anytime soon.

With nervous hands he reached forward and pulled the door open in one quick move.

'Natalie?' he called, his voice wavering.

When no response came he entered the building. The room was dimly lit by an all but useless strip light above and several candles precariously balanced on a crate acting as a table. A quick check revealed no evidence of Natalie, or Maggie Dean.

His heart sank.

Then he felt the stab of something hard in the centre of his back.

Chapter 59

'Well aren't you resourceful?' the voice of Maggie Dean said, barely disguising her delight. Harry went to turn, wanting to face his aggressor and a woman who had out-smarted him from the start, but he felt the sharp prod of what he assumed was a hand gun pressing into the small of his back and remained eyes front.

'You're a hard lady to find, do you know that?' the investigator replied, his eyes searching the dimly lit room for any sign of a weapon.

'I've been closer than you think, at all times.'

'Send my regards to Derek Mayhew the next time you speak to him.' Harry's tone of voice held a mixture of annoyance and amusement.

'Thought you would have cottoned on sooner but then again you did have your hands full elsewhere didn't you?' Harry remained silent, ignoring the implications to Natalie and to the fact that he had taken his eyes off the job in hand, that he had let his professionalism become clouded. It was something that niggled at him; it was why they were in this predicament now.

'Cat got your tongue?' she said, goading him into a response that was not forthcoming. From behind he felt a push as his body was sent reeling forward, collapsing to the ground as his feet slid over bits of cardboard and causing dust moats to rise in the air. He landed in a heap not far from where he had previously stood.

Ahead of him stood Maggie Dean; Natalie was to her side, her hands behind her back no doubt cuffed or tied with rope. Her face was pale, her eyes wide with fear and her cheeks stained with tears; otherwise she looked unharmed, physically. It was a small mercy he was thankful for.

Natalie's eyes met his, they were reaching out to him silently, looking for a sign that everything was going to be fine, that this situation would work out, that they would somehow survive this madness.

Harry offered a half smile as hope, it was all he had.

Maggie chuckled, the sound echoing around the room.

'How sweet it is,' she said, looking from one to the other. 'How does George feel about you fucking his beloved daughter?' Maggie finished, edging forward slightly, the gun still pointed in the vague direction of the fallen investigator, her voice etched with a harder tone. 'Looks as though it will be a brief affair though.' With that she raised the gun and slid her finger over the trigger.

The time for talking was over.

The time for action was upon her.

It was time to end the games.

Suddenly Maggie was knocked from her feet as Natalie slammed her body into the side of her captor. The woman went sprawling, knocking into a crate that was being used as a candle stand. Both the candle and its holder fell from the crate instantly setting ablaze a pile of cardboard and stacked papers that had managed to keep some of the damp at bay. The gun discharged with a deafening roar along with a flash of light.

Chapter 60

The smell of the fired weapon hung in the air and mingled with the burning cardboard and paper. Harry struggled to his feet as quickly as he could whilst the fallen form of Maggie Dean was momentarily incapacitated. In the fall the gun had left her hand and was now lying hidden by the darkness of the room. Whilst searching frantically for her weapon Harry was upon her.

He grabbed her, slammed her against the rear wall, winding her as he did so.

She was surprised, her mouth forming soundless words as he helped Natalie to her feet and moved her towards the door, out of harm's way.

Snarling like a rabid dog, cursing and spitting words, her eyes wide with anger, Maggie Dean made to grab at the investigator but he was too quick. He sidestepped her and with a gentle nudge to her back sent her flying to the floor.

'Harry,' Natalie cried, her eyes leading him to the lost gun. Quickly he crouched down and clasped the weapon in his hand. Up on his feet he turned from a crouch to full height, the gun pointing towards the now standing Maggie Dean.

'Wait there Maggie; come any closer and I promise I'll shoot you where you stand.'

'You haven't got the guts Harry.' Her voice was calm again, under control despite the position she found herself in. The tables were turned, it grated on her. She looked to her sister with eyes that flashed with hatred, pure and simple.

Maggie Dean bit down on her lip in frustration and then made her decision; she had no other choice. She started to move forward, looking to run at Harry Stone, ready to barge into his body.

Stone didn't blink, he just fired the gun.

Chapter 61

The old farmhouse was lit up as though daylight had come early. Police officers, a fire crew and members of the ambulance response team milled around with the team of crime scene investigators like extras on a movie set. Blue lights flashed silently and for the first time the whispering of the trees could not compete and were drowned out to mere background noise.

Detective Inspector Tony Scott stood outside what remained of the outbuilding talking frantically into his mobile phone whilst he surveyed the scene around him. As he ended the call he walked across to the rear of an ambulance, Harry Stone stood there flanking the dark haired woman, Natalie Soderman, who was wrapped in a blanket, her face as white as a ghost, the smell of smoke lingering in the air.

George Soderman had already been taken to hospital, a place he had only hours ago left, only this time he returned with a gun shot wound to the leg, otherwise unharmed and stable, if not in total shock.

'Harry.' The DI said, wiping a hand over a tired face. 'Can I have a word?' Both men left Natalie to the waiting servicemen. 'I'm going to have to get a statement from you, Miss Soderman and her father.'

'Can it wait until tomorrow?'

'I guess so; I can send patrol round in the morning.'

'Thanks Tony, appreciate it.'

'Do you know who the second guy in the cellar was?'

'No idea, sorry.'

'No matter, we'll run his details, I'm sure he'll turn up on the system someplace.'

'Is that it, can I take Natalie to the hospital now to see her father?'

'Yeah sure, we've got some work to do here. Once Maggie Dean is patched up we'll interview her; nice shooting by the way.'

Harry smiled and gently patted the DI on the shoulder and began walking back towards Natalie.

'Hey Harry?' the investigator stopped and looked over his shoulder. 'Why the hell didn't you call me when this started getting out of hand?'

'I thought about it, trust me. Next time you'll be the first one I call.'

'Next time, I thought you specialised in missing persons not psychotic gun-toting sisters.'

Both men exchanged a smile before the DI watched Harry return to Natalie's side.

* * *

Harry took the bottle of Jim Beam from the cupboard and poured himself two fingers worth before drinking down the burning liquid in one go. From the lounge came the low hum of the television, a twenty-four hour news channel was on, the presenters eulogising on the financial crisis that was happening in Greece and Spain. Wandering through, the investigator kicked off his shoes and collapsed into his chair.

George Soderman was still in hospital, his daughter at his side. Natalie had promised to ring when she had some news.

His mobile phone began ringing and Harry remembered that his phone had rung earlier and ever since the voicemail service had been ringing him back, reminding him of the message that had been left. He scrolled through the numbers and found the voicemail number, pressed redial and waited for the message to play.

Sara's voice cut through the madness of the evening.

She wanted to meet with him, had something she needed to discuss. Tired and weary, Harry made a mental note to contact her tomorrow and arrange a meeting.

Chapter 62

Harry sat on the bench in *The Gardens* lost in thought. According to the weather report he had seen in the morning, the day had promised to be unseasonably warm, but what had been promised had definitely not been delivered. Above him the grey skies looked unmovable with the biting chill of winter, the warm spell nothing more than a dream that would not come to fruition for another five months, if they were lucky.

As his eyes trailed the sky above, Harry became aware of a presence close by.

Someone sat down next to him, unspeaking, revelling in the silence.

Harry turned to see Detective Inspector Tony Scott sat next to him.

'Are you stalking me now?' Harry asked, smiling as both men looked out over the peacefulness of the gardens. Both of their chosen professions found them brushing and, more often than not, colliding with the very darkness that mankind offered, whilst at the same time bringing hope to the hopeless and safety to the vulnerable. Harry Stone and DI Tony Scott were two different men from two different walks of life running against a similar tide.

'Thought you might want to know the latest on Maggie Dean?' Harry's smile vanished, replaced by a more sober appearance.

'So what is the latest?' the investigator asked after a few moments of silence.

'She is as quiet as a damn mouse, won't say a word. Just sits there and stares into blankness.' Harry laughed, but the sound contained no hint of amusement, moreover the complete opposite.

'You think she will talk?'

'Eventually, those sort always do, just a matter of time my friend. How have things been?'

'Crazy to tell you the truth.'

'I heard there was a lot of interest in you and your company and your services, at least work won't be slow for a while.' Harry laughed again; the detective didn't know the half of it. 'I also heard that a certain Miss Fox is almost stalking you for an interview.'

'Every day I have some kind of message asking for a meeting, or a conference call.'

'Good looking woman by all accounts.' Scott said, resisting the urge to say anything further. He had come up against Vicki Fox several times in the last few years himself. She was a freelance reporter and investigator who was a tenacious and persistent reporter with a doggedness that was both respected and feared in equal measure. A frequent contributor for many of the daily newspapers she could also be seen writing articles for many of the weekend supplements as well as magazines such as *Wired*, *Cosmopolitan* and *The Economist*.

A stunningly beautiful woman, Vicki Fox was a woman who always got her man.

Harry Stone laughed, felt the biting chill of the day seep through his coat.

'Well I can't sit around here all day chatting to you, seems I have a lot of paperwork to be sorting out thanks to you.' Scott said with a smile as he pushed himself up off the seat. He held out his hand towards Stone which the investigator stood to meet. 'Next time give me the heads up yeah.' It was not a question and Stone took the meaning as both men went their separate ways.

* * *

George Soderman had locked himself away in his study on the pretence of clearing his desk and tidying through his multitude of papers. If the truth be known he was most likely having a sleep in his chair whilst Billie Holiday played from the stereo, relieved to be out of hospital and home again. He was relieved to have this nightmare now safely behind him and equally happy to be alive as well as his daughter. For a time there, whilst he had been slumped beneath the floor, he had wondered if that was to be it, if he would bow out in the dark with an unknown cellmate for company and the dread of not knowing what was happening to Natalie.

Each time he closed his eyes he was sent back there, back to that dark and dank cell that was to have been his final destination, his ultimate resting place. It would have been too, had it not been for Harry Stone who, despite concerns that he had taken his eye off the ball in favour of his daughter, the man had come through.

* * *

Natalie stood on the front step watching as Harry climbed out of his car then made his way across to greet her. He carried a bunch of flowers in one hand a bottle in the other. His face broke out in a smile the instant he saw Natalie.

'Welcome back stranger,' she said, kissing him deeply on the mouth, her tongue probing his, her hands reaching around his back as she pulled him in tight to her body as though they had been apart for months. 'How did it go?' she asked, referring to his coffee with Sara.

Harry smiled and leant in to kiss Natalie.

'Fine, she just wanted to let me know that she was getting married, wanted to tell me instead of having me find out some other way.'

'That's nice. You okay about it?'

'Yeah I'm fine.' They hugged some more and shared a longer, deeper kiss. It had been a quick coffee with Sara, half an hour no more, and then they had been going their separate ways, this time forever. For the first time Harry had watched his ex walk away without the slightest hint of loss or pang of guilt. They had left on good terms and he honestly wished her well in her new life; it was a sign that he took to be good.

'Hey, watch the flowers. You know how upset George gets if I give him damaged flowers.' She laughed and smacked him playfully on the arm before leading him in through the front door. In the kitchen he placed the flowers and the bottle on the side then turned to face her before enveloping her in his arms once more.

In the week that had gone since Harry Stone had ended Maggie Dean's vendetta against her sister, there had been endless questions by the police and reporters alike. He had appeared on local radio as well as the local regional edition of the news. Interest in Harry Stone had gone through the roof; as a marketing campaign it was a winner. It seemed as though everyone now wanted a piece of the shy and retiring private investigator. He had even had a call from someone who worked for Gates, Stone and Moseley, a local marketing company, asking if he wanted to meet to discuss any possible business. Harry said he would get back to them, wondering if perhaps it wasn't a bad idea getting a proper marketing firm on board. He had also thought about the hiring of a junior investigator more seriously. So much so that next week he was interviewing a man called John Ratcliffe; it was a step in the right direction. His assistant couldn't run everything whilst Harry was off on jobs, and besides, Laurence Hunter had taken a young Harry Stone into his fold years ago, perhaps now was the time to return the favour and give someone else the opportunity and the chance.

Harry kissed Natalie once more on the cheek.

'You sounded all mysterious on the phone, so what's up?'

'Are you all set?'

'Yes, but what's going on?' Harry took Natalie by the hand, shouted his goodbyes to George Soderman as he guided the woman towards the front door, giving her time only to grab her coat and keys before whisking her outside towards his car. As they sat in the car, the engine idling, the radio playing the final few verses of some folk-rock classic, Harry turned to Natalie and smiled, glad that it was all over.

'I think I still owe you a meal.'

Epilogue

The interview room was cemetery still, the silence oppressive.

The girl who sat at the table tapped her fingernails against the table top as though keeping in time to an unheard beat. She was aware that behind the mirror men were watching her, observing her like a laboratory rat waiting to see if the experiment had worked.

She probably didn't need to tell them that it had failed.

Maggie hadn't uttered a word since being brought in. She had kept her council as she had always planned to.

The silence frustrated them, annoyed them.

To her it was mere amusement. They were so easy to play with, but then again most men were.

It wouldn't be long before Detective Inspector Scott would return, his exasperation for the moment held in check despite the reddening of his face and the continuous crunching of his knuckles. He would sit down and ask his pointless questions over and over, always in the hope that she would begin to talk. Always anticipating the moment when she would break her self imposed silence and gloat in her plans, her murders, her grand scheme.

He would look into her eyes and try and guess what was happening inside of her mind, but he would find nothing, he would get no answers. Not now, not ever.

Maggie thought back to her early therapy sessions with Dr Fox. In those initial sessions when she would sit in silence, keep her council and watch with amusement as the frustration began to grow moment by moment, until Fox would pace the room in barely disguised annoyance whilst always trying to give off an air of calmness.

She stifled a yawn, bored with their games.

She stood up, the first movement since she had been brought into the room. Maggie wondered if now they were all alert, speculating if this was the moment.

She walked over to the two way mirror with her best poker face.

She cupped her hands above her eyes and peered in as though a great light was being shone over her face. She tilted her head this way and that, playing with them, toying like a cat with a mouse before the final killer pounce.

And then she turned and looked dead centre into the mirror.

Let out a laugh, a deep guttural teasing giggle that echoed around the room.

As quickly as the sound had been there, it was gone.

She walked back over to the chair, sat down and resumed her tap-tap-tapping against the table top.

CPSIA information can be obtained at www.ICGtesting.com
Printed in the USA
BVOW021052230512

290925BV00015B/64/P